The Later People

By

Mary C. Bodel, MH

Copyright June 2019

2090 the Tech No Tribe

"Thanksgiving was awesome," Alex told the committee. "You're right, having parties does make things better."

"You haven't seen anything yet," Brandon chuckled. "Now we start prepping for Christmas."

"What, aside from the religious aspect, makes Christmas different?"

"We do Twelfth Night," Henrietta said. "Brandon and Trevor were the Lords of Misrule last year. Alderson had the year before that and Nelson did the first one. Reilly, I think it's your turn."

"Me? How can I do a job like that?" Reilly sputtered.

"Same way we did it," Nelson said. "Talk to people. Some events have become traditional so you'll have some patterns to follow. Get creative. Do something no one has thought of."

"I think I can but I'm going to have to talk to a lot of people," Reilly said. "Can we talk about decorations and trees now? Those I can wrap my head around."

"Enough snow has melted that we can get some trees and a yule log," Brandon said. "Jeannie, are there any storms coming in the next two weeks?"

"We might get some rain in a couple of days but no snow in the near future. I've read about Twelfth Night, this sounds like fun."

"It is," Brandon said. "We'll schedule getting greenery later as we don't want it to dry out. In the meantime we're going to all be busy making or trading for gifts. Matt, you and Henrietta have already started, right?"

"Yes we have. I've got a bunch of volunteers trading time for gifts. Some may turn out to be fairly good carvers. We've even made some blocks for Emma to play with."

"We've got dolls, fancy clothing has been ordered and like Matt I have a lot of volunteers. Some can only sew on a button or stuff a rag doll but there are others that may be joining the team. Several are competent in sewing and a few have taken a liking to weaving."

"Good. Aside from what we've already traded for is there a way we can make candy for the kids?" Brandon asked.

"Grandma showed us how to make molasses candy and something she calls divinity. We have the ingredients plus we can make rock candy," Annette replied.

"I'm glad you said 'us,'" Brandon said.

"Yeah, making candy can mean being on my feet a lot. There are other things I can do and mostly I'm supervising right now as we have enough other chefs."

"How are you doing, James?" Brandon asked.

"I have volunteers but none interested in metal work except Trevor. I think he wants to know how to do everything. Most of the requests I have are for jewelry or fancy boxes which will probably be for jewelry."

"I like the pins you made for last year's scavenger hunt," Reilly said. "Any chance of a repeat?"

James grinned. "Yes, I think I can do that. Those are easy."

"I hope we aren't giving out tongue depressors this year," Dr. Mike said. "I'd rather it be something useful."

"How about a small first aid kit?" Brandon suggested. "I've been thinking about that a lot and there have been plenty of times when it would have come in handy."

"What would you put in it?" Henrietta asked.

"Simple stuff such as bandages, willow bark capsules, tweezers for splinters and maybe a small bottle of the oil."

"I can make you small bandage rolls if that would help," Henrietta said.

"I'll make the tweezers," James said. "They aren't hard and maybe one of the volunteers will take an interest."

"I can make up more capsules and oil," Brandon said. "I'm not sure what to put the oil in, though."

"We have a lot of small jars in the kitchen. They're a little smaller than what baby food jars looked like before cryo. They have screw on lids, too," Annette said. "We'll want to trade for more next time because they hold just the right amount for the few babies we have, which is what we've been using them for."

"Do you have enough so that the little ones won't be deprived?" Brandon asked.

"Yes or I wouldn't have said anything. Even if we didn't have them we have enough other dishes."

"I'll have to think of something for the animals," Amaya said. "I don't think my arm is up to making straw hearts this year."

"How about feathers?" Cindy asked. "We've got them from the ducks and the chickens."

"Do you think there are enough?" Amaya asked.

"If not I have plenty and who needs to know where they came from," Henrietta said. "We need your arm to heal and it's been less than a week since you broke it."

"That makes sense," Amaya said. "It's a relief to know I can still participate."

"I think I'll stick to wood shavings," Matt said. "We have those in plenty and with all the orders we have it would be hard to make something else."

"That's fine and I suggest the kitchen stick with cookies," Brandon said. "Anyone else you draft won't be on the council but that's just as well. I'd like there to be a few surprises."

Christmas Eve

"I'm glad the snow held off long enough for us to get everything in," Trevor said as he helped haul the yule log onto the porch. "I like white Christmases but preferably not hunting for decorations in it."

"What happens next?" Alex asked, dusting off his hands.

"Next we have a Christmas Eve service for those who want to attend. That's usually everyone but it's optional. Keeping grounded in our faith is important."

"I definitely want to attend. I wonder if they'll do a Nativity scene."

"I suspect so but the only baby we have is Emma and I'm not real sure she'll stay in a manger. She's walking some now."

"I don't care; it's who the baby represents that's important."

After the service Brandon and Annette collected their children.

"I can't believe Emma stayed in the manger that whole time," Brandon said.

"She was sleepy, though she didn't quite go to sleep. Petey looked so cute and Mikey did a good job."

"Yes, you boys did very well," Brandon said. "Are you ready to go outside and sing some carols?"

"Yes!" Mikey said, which Petey echoed.

As they were standing outside singing Brandon noticed Abe picking something up. He carefully hid it in his parka and continued on with the caroling. When they were done and most people had gotten their cookies and coco he showed it to Brandon.

"After they all go to bed we need to have a council meeting. I've never seen an arrow like this one."

"It certainly isn't one of ours. Any idea how long it's been there?"

"It didn't have a lot of snow on it. I'm surprised the sentries didn't see anything. That's worrisome."

"It's a dark night and the arrow is black. See if you can get it into the council chamber. I'd rather we do the rest of the evening before we talk about it."

"Will do. Maybe I should go up and warn the sentries…"

"That's probably a good idea. They all know not to say anything until we do."

After all had gone to bed, the council met before the fire.

"I recognize that arrow," Benton said. "It is the other tribe that Ruth mentioned. They do not like others in their territory."

"Are we in their territory?" Brandon asked. "I would think we'd have noticed."

"Not unless they have recently moved to this area. Have they ever bothered the Camps?" Benton asked Brin.

"No. I've never seen an arrow like it and it would surely have been brought to my grandfather."

"Perhaps that's why they didn't continue an attack," Annette suggested.

"If they are moving to this area they may be telling us that they don't want us here," Benton said. "They don't have a problem moving into someone else's territory. They had to be taught respect for ours but that was in my father's time so I don't remember a lot about it."

"Why is the arrow all black?" Bob asked.

"They use arrows that blend in with the surroundings. It is a dark night so a black arrow would be hard to see until it came into light. It landed in the darkness and might not even have been seen until the snow melted had you not gone outside to sing. Remind me later to ask you more about that," Benton concluded.

"So in a blizzard we could expect them to be white and in a forest brown and/or green?" Abe asked. "Clever if you want to fool a human. Wasteful unless you have some sort of religious belief otherwise."

"Their religion is strange. We believe they could have all of the things you do but for religious reasons don't use them. Their bows are as advanced as yours, as are the arrows. They do not ride horses nor keep animals, but again it appears to be related to their belief system. Ruth could tell you more."

"I'll radio Home Base tomorrow and ask," Brandon said. "For now do you think we are in danger of attack?"

"No. They do not like being out in bad weather. Did you not say a storm was coming tomorrow?" Benton asked Jeannie.

"Yes, it should last two days. It will hit sometime after breakfast but from what I've heard most activities for the next two days are all indoor, so other than caring for the animals we'd be ok."

"All right. In that case, merry Christmas and for those unfamiliar, welcome to Twelfth Night," Brandon said. "Annette and I have a little Santa playing of our own to do."

Christmas Day

"Mommy! Daddy! Santa came!" Mikey squealed as he jumped up and down.

"Yeah, Santa," Petey repeated.

Brandon yawned. "He did? What did he bring?"

"We got candy and a horse with a cart, one for me and one for Petey and we got clothes. They're fancy but they look funny. They also look comfortable," Mikey said, holding up a Renaissance outfit.

"They should be," Annette said, quickly changing Emma and putting on her new dress. "Are you ready for breakfast?"

"Can I bring my new toy?" Mikey asked.

"I think you might want to leave it here," Brandon said. "I heard something about him making a stop in the common room so there might be other things for you."

"Really? We are really getting Christmas!!" the excited little boy said.

The family went down to breakfast. Mikey and Petey joined the other wide eyed children receiving gifts from the tree.

"Mommy, look at this airplane!" Mikey exclaimed.

"I got horsie," Petey said although Brandon had to carry the rocking horse. Emma promptly put one of her blocks in her mouth.

"Now that the presents have all been given out do you think you could eat some breakfast?" Annette asked with a laugh.

"Yes, I'm hungry. What are we having?" Mikey said.

"I believe that a couple of the chefs have tried making Grandma's famous breakfast ring," Brandon said with a slight blush. "Merideth and Trevor helped."

"This is good," Annette said. "It's also nice to have a tradition to follow."

"We'll have several," Brandon said with a grin. "I think our Lord of Misrule is about to begin."

"Ladies and gentlemen, young and old I am your Lord of Misrule!" Reilly cried.

"What's a Lord of Misrule?" Mikey asked.

"He gets to make and/or change rules for the next twelve days," Annette whispered. "It's a lot of fun."

"Indeed, Annette, it shall be," Reilly said, having heard both question and answer. "First the traditional abolishments. No mandatory naps and no bedtimes. Also, no school until the festivities are over!"

After the clapping died down he continued. "There will be times when the adults may freely indulge in a nap while our children are otherwise occupied. The first will begin in about an hour. You may wish to use this time to prepare for another tradition...the funny hat contest!

"This year we have a theme. Fad hats from before we went cryo."

"Where did he come up with that?" Annette asked as they went back to put the children's toys away.

"We told him to use his imagination," Brandon replied. "I'm glad I have a sombrero. I can decorate that a bit. What are you going to wear?"

"Grandma made both Emma and me sunbonnets. A few decorations and we should be good to go. I'm not out to win a contest but having something suitable and different is nice."

"I'm glad Mikey and Petey will be making their own. That's always a fun activity. I helped a bit last year."

"I'm just wondering what dance he could possibly come up with. We've done all of the crazy ones I can think of," Annette said.

"We'll find out after the hat contest," Brandon said with a grin. "While the kids get ready I'm going to check with the sentries. I want to keep an eye out for more arrows."

"Hi, Brandon," Abe said. "How's Reilly doing?"

"So far he's doing a good job. The funny hat contest has a theme this year."

"Yeah, I heard. I'm kind of glad to be out here for that one. I'm also glad to miss whatever the dance is."

"Reilly obviously has it planned. Any movement or signs of more arrows?"

"No, but as Jeannie said it's snowing pretty hard. If they're smart they went back to whatever camp they had."

"You know, it struck me that the arrow came from the area where the avalanche happened. You don't suppose they hid in there to watch and shoot?"

"If they were on the far side it would be hard to see them. However that would put them in considerable danger."

"If they're new to this area I don't think they'd know. They may not have seen an avalanche before."

"They should have seen debris slides, they aren't new."

"Maybe, maybe not. This is the first area where we've found evidence of regular slides. It's also the first area we've moved into that had a strip mine near it. Who knows what the years have done to other areas."

"We'll have to keep an eye out and I suppose if there's another avalanche we're going to have to go and see if we can rescue them."

"What would Benton say? We Wakers are strange people. We help our enemies rather than kill them."

"What else can we do?" Abe said with a sigh. "It's just how we are."

"Time for me to go and help Annette with the kids, and then she's going to help make lunch. We've already got our hats figured out."

"That's good. I'm betting this will be hilarious."

As everyone entered the dining hall for lunch they were sporting their hats.

"What kind of hat are you wearing?" Brandon asked Mikey.

"Henrietta and her team made a bunch of straw hats for us to decorate. I used ribbon and feathers," Mikey said. "Then I helped Petey. He added holly and ivy."

"They look very nice," Annette said.

"What are you wearing?" Mikey asked Annette. "I've never seen a hat like that before."

"Emma and I are wearing sunbonnets. I think we're the only two in the contest, which should prove interesting. Daddy is wearing a sombrero that Henrietta made for him after he got sunburned really bad helping in the garden."

"I like all the feathers. I think it's the best hat in here," Mikey said.

"We'll find out soon," Brandon replied. "Our Lord of Misrule is ready to make announcements."

"Ladies and gentlemen, the awards for our contest are as follows: all of the children have won prizes. A special prize goes to Mikey for helping his brother with the rather prickly details of Petey's hat. For the adults we have the rarity of a couple. Brandon, you and Annette have the two most unique hats.

"Other prizes go to Amaya for the Victorian lady's style, Cindy for the pill box version of a hat and Trevor for finding a way to make a fisherman's hat using a straw base.

"Now for the dance!"

The adults groaned.

"We're going to do the Hokey Pokey!"

"Hey, I know how to do that one," Mikey said.

"Most of us do. Some of us have even done it on roller skates," Brandon replied. "It could be worse."

"What would be worse?" Annette asked.

"We did the Funky Chicken the first year."

"Yeah. That would qualify as worse."

Reilly had several groups of circles for the dance. The kids laughed when the adults had to 'put their backsides in and shake them all about.'

"Ok. Maybe the Funky Chicken was better," Brandon muttered when the dance was over.

"At least I'm not the only pregnant woman that had to stick a bulging tummy in and shake it all about," Annette said. "The baby seems to like it; I'm getting kicked right now."

"Next up are games!" Reilly announced.

"Not for us," Annette said. "We need to head for the kitchen."

"I'll keep an eye on the kids," Merideth said. "Is Emma going to the nursery?"

"Yes, she's about ready for a nap, mandatory or not," Annette said. "I'll drop her off before I start cooking."

"I'm glad you actually started yesterday," Brandon said when she came into the kitchen. "Are you making Grandma's soup?"

"I am indeed. What are you making?"

"Shrimp with confetti pasta for those who can't or won't eat fish and bacon wrapped trout for those who do. Both are easy and fast but I'll have to do the pasta first."

It didn't take Brandon long to finish his contributions to the feast so he was ready when the next round of football was to be played.

"Congratulations, Brandon. You will be in the finals come New Year's Day," Reilly said at the end of the contest. "Now for the feast!"

Benton chose a seat next to Brandon.

"As I said last night I have some questions. The service you held is very similar to something we believe. Is this something that came from before?"

"Yes, it is. The celebration of the birth of Jesus, who would have been called something similar to Joshua, became tradition after His death and resurrection. While we still don't know for sure how long we were in cryo sleep it would now be about two thousand two hundred years since His birth."

"We believe in a Man who died for us that we might know the Father and rose so that we might rise at the end of days."

"It is the same Man. He died for our sins so that we could communicate with God, our Father and rose so that we will be able to rise and live with Him for eternity."

"You don't force people to believe this?"

"No, we don't. We try to live so that those who don't know Him want to. Most do."

"Is that why you have such strange ways? Healing your enemies and giving things to those who are in need?"

"That is exactly why. Jesus said that people will know that we follow Him because of the love we show to those around us. Not just our friends and family but strangers and even enemies."

"What will you do to these people of the painted arrows?"

"We will do the same thing we've always done. We will protect ourselves but we will try for nonviolence. If we find one of them hurt we will care for them, even if they betray us in return."

"Beware because these people will."

"That's between them and God."

"Your strange ways make more sense now. I will adopt them even though I was trained to kill my enemies."

"You are a wise man, Benton."

"What are you going to do if there are more arrows?"

"This time we'll find where they hid and follow the tracks. We need to know more about them."

"With those boards of yours you should be able to do so but they do not like change. I don't know how they'd react to your technology."

"If they don't have any we have the edge."

Christmas dinner was one of the longer feasts served throughout the year and by the time it was over the children were nearly asleep. Because the festivities were as much about relationship building between relative strangers younger children were to sleep in the daycare facility so the adults could mingle. Brandon and Annette took the sleepy children and kissed them goodnight before seeing what Reilly would be up to.

"Ladies and gentlemen, tonight's game is going to be simple. It's called Rainbow Bingo. I didn't think we'd want to use a lot of brain power after such a hearty meal."

"What's Rainbow Bingo?" Janet asked.

"I'm glad you asked. There will be six groups. Each group will be assigned an area of the common room, kitchen or dining room. Each person will be handed a bingo card. There are twelve colors on the card and twelve identical crayons hidden in the areas.

"You will go in ten at a time and the first person who gets all twelve colors will remain to offer hints to other players. In the end, all of those who finished first will have a playoff game."

"What are the rest of us going to do while we wait?" Jax asked.

"Talk to your fellow team mates. There are refreshments of various kinds for us to enjoy during the evening. By the way, put your crayon back where you found it when done," Reilly added.

As the first group went in Brin came to talk to Cindy. "Is this a common game?"

"No, it's the first time I ever heard of it but it sounds like fun," she said. "Have you had some of the root beer?"

"Yes. I must say I like it better than that clear sort of liquid."

"That's probably a good thing. I like wine but too much of it and I'm not going to be able to walk let alone play games."

"This is a most unusual festival. Do you always celebrate together, men, women and children?"

"Yes, especially at this time of year. This is my second year awake and the Wakers have found that having many celebrations during the cold and snowy months helps prevent people from sleeping too much or getting upset."

"The Camps would benefit from that. I'm sure Billy and Mirin will guide them in that direction. It is good that we have all declared peace and become allies."

"You are next in line to be leader of the Camps."

"No. I am one of the Wakers now. I made that commitment when I decided to join this community. My grandfather approves.

"Once I only sought glory, especially for me. Now I seek peace and security for all of us."

"You are a good man, Brin and a great warrior."

Brin blushed.

The results of the contest had Benton, Janet and a very surprised Brin taking the top three spots.

Sleigh Rides and Arrows

After breakfast Reilly stood up to announce the day's plan.

"First off we will be having sleigh rides. This may take most of the day but this afternoon the children will be having games while the adults take a rest."

Brandon and Annette were in the last group to go for a ride. Because Little Charlie had toppled out of the sleigh the year before Petey and Emma stayed in the nursery. Mikey was thrilled to have his parents to himself.

"Are we going to see anything exciting?" he asked.

"You never know," Brandon said. "Last year Jackie and her family saw a mountain lion get a deer and Cindy got to see where the beavers live."

While the ride itself was mostly uneventful halfway back Brandon heard a thunk in the wood of the cart. Glancing behind he decided to keep driving rather than retrieve the white arrow sticking out of the rear section of the cart.

"You should get out on mommy's side," Brandon told Mikey after pulling up close to the ground sentry point. "I think you might find some hot chocolate waiting for you."

Annette gave Brandon a look before taking the boy inside. Abe was examining the arrow almost before the two got into the house.

"Same make, different color," Abe said. "Who do you want to suit up?"

"I'd go but I think that would cause more problems," Brandon said. "We'll need Trevor. Who else can we send?"

"Henry. He's good and he's single. Where did you get hit?"

"Along the fence line close to where the avalanche ended. They are using that zone."

"I'll send them out. We'll meet after Reilly calls for the kids to play games and the adults rest. You should probably let Annette know what happened because she knows something did."

"Yeah. I couldn't tell her then because I didn't want Mikey to know. First it would scare him and second he'd probably say something."

"We may have to say something anyway."

Annette was waiting just outside the daycare door. "What happened?" she asked.

Brandon explained and she nodded. "I'm glad you didn't say anything because it would have scared Mikey. I'm getting scared. What is being done?"

"Trevor and Henry are investigating. When the adult rest time is announced we'll have a council meeting. By then we may have more information."

An hour later the council met with Trevor included.

"We found where they shot from," Trevor said. "There were two of them. They tried to disguise that by the one following stepping into the leader's foot tracks but they had to switch. That's how we figured out how many they were."

"Where were they?" Brandon asked.

"Along one of the gulches in the avalanche zone," Henry replied. "They seem to have left right after the shot. We followed about three miles but the tracks kept going. It's getting ready to snow again so we came back."

"Wherever they are camping is some distance from us, then," Benton said. "I wonder why they are shooting at us."

"We use things they don't," Brin said. "We have horses and carts. We have electricity. We have warm houses that do not require a fire."

"They're jealous?" Abe asked.

"I do not think so. Just as we believed in the Ancient Ones who did not turn out to be precisely what we expected they may not believe in the use of these things. They have not hit a person but they have aimed at things."

"That first arrow could have been aimed at a porch light," Abe said. "There wasn't anyone out there when it was fired."

"They could have shot one of us," Brandon added. "It hit on my side but fairly far back."

"I'd hate to see their reaction to a hover cart," Annette said. "Maybe we should ask Gavin what to do in case an arrow does hit one."

"I'd rather do that in private and not in council," Brandon said. "Brin's theory is sound but I think we still need more information.

"Reilly, is what you've got planned for tomorrow inside?"

“It can be. It’ll take some work.”

Day Three

"As today is another snow day we shall have indoor activities," Reilly announced after breakfast. "I have decided we will do a talent show this year just as was done the first year. Today you will be divided into two groups.

"One group will put their names in my hat and the other will draw names out of it. That will be your partner for the show. You should spend the first part of the day working out what you might perform together."

"Who will judge the contest?" Jackie asked.

"I have selected a panel," Reilly said mysteriously.

"Yeah, I'm on it," Annette whispered to Brandon. "He's concerned that pregnant women might get hurt."

"Several council members are on it," Brandon whispered back. "Not all of us but there are enough that we can respond to a problem should one arise."

"I hadn't thought of that, plus a talent show is something that could keep us occupied safely indoors if needs be."

As they were talking the names were being drawn.

"What is a talent show?" Brin asked Cindy when she drew his name.

"Yes, we'd like to know as well," Thi and Ally asked. Ally had drawn Thi.

"It's where we talk about the things we can do and then do them in front of everybody. It can be funny, serious and/or dramatic," Cindy replied. "As an example I can play the recorder. Do you have a talent, Brin?"

"We aren't encouraged to develop that sort of thing but we do learn histories and have story tellers. I have studied with them."

"I could play music in the background appropriate to the story. See, we already have an act."

"Ours would have to be weapons related," Ally said. "I could tell stories but Thi doesn't play an instrument. He is more agile but I am not."

"We can figure that out," Thi said.

Conversations of this nature were going on all around the common room. Reilly smiled, pleased to see that many of the pairings had people that didn't know one another well working together. After an hour he clapped his hands for attention.

"There will be more time to discuss your acts during the children's play period… unless you prefer a nap," he said when the room had quieted. "For now we are going to play hide and seek in rounds."

The children squealed with delight while some of the adults groaned. At the end of the game Brandon was the loser and had to don the hat Henrietta had made the previous year.

"At least it looks good on me," he said to Annette.

After lunch the children had their craft time. Brandon went to talk to the weather forecasters.

"This storm seems to be dryer than the last one. Is that going to pose a problem?" he asked.

"It can," Jeannie answered, "and you're right. It's colder so the snow is dryer. It probably won't adhere very well to what's already on the ground. It could slide soon or it could hold off for another storm and then slide."

"How many storms are lined up?"

"It's probably going to be every two or three days and it will be a mix of snow types. An Alberta Clipper is funneling down and meeting up with a warm, moist air from the west. If I had access to ocean temperatures in the Pacific I'd guess there's an El Nino out there."

"So it's going to be a very snowy winter."

"Yes and that's even if we don't have any more nor'easters."

"Should we cause a planned avalanche?"

"Only if you know there wouldn't be anyone in the path."

Brandon nodded. While he was glad she hadn't mentioned why there might be, creating a situation where someone might be injured or killed didn't seem like a good idea.

After this conversation he headed for the kitchen.

"You're not scheduled to cook today," Annette said.

"No, but I just got the weather report. Tomorrow should be clear so you may want to stock up. There are a line of snowstorms heading our way and any one of them could set off another avalanche. That won't affect us but it might be safer to not have to go back and forth getting supplies."

"Good idea. Reilly is planning snow sculptures for tomorrow and a backwards dinner tomorrow night. He's also setting aside time for the contestants to practice as the first round of competition will be day after tomorrow."

"Sounds good. I'd like to keep everyone on the opposite side of the buildings just in case though I think Brin's theory is sound."

"Have you talked to Gavin yet?"

"About?"

"The hover carts. What would an arrow do to them?"

"I had better do that now before I forget again."

"He's probably in the garage," Annette said.

Brandon went out to the garage and found Gavin busy working on one of the hover carts.

"What are you fixing?" Brandon asked.

"I got a message from Home Base about a button we hadn't been able to figure out. Did you know these things and those boards have a sort of force field?"

"No, but it may solve the problem I was going to ask you about."

"What problem? I got the feeling that the message I received was because of something the council told Home Base."

"You would be accurate and I think you probably should join the council. We're going to need your information and what we already know could help you protect us and our technology.

"On Christmas Eve Abe found a spent arrow in the snow where we went out to sing Christmas carols. Yesterday another arrow hit the cart I was driving during the sleigh ride. It's thought that the people firing the arrows don't like or approve of things of a mechanical nature. A hover cart is sure to freak them out."

"Yeah, and the boards. Plus with the boards they could hit the rider. I'll continue my tests and report to the council this evening. That's when you guys meet, right?"

"That's right. After whatever game Reilly has planned for us."

"He sure is coming up with some doozies. I haven't played hide and seek since I was a kid and it's probably been at least that long since I've used a crayon."

The game of the evening was charades. Brandon redeemed himself by winning and Leon found himself wearing the hat. After that the council headed for the chamber. When they arrived they found that Jeannie had a little presentation for them.

"Brandon asked me about the possibility of more avalanches in the area we've now set as off limits. I thought it might help if you understood a little about the mechanics of an avalanche.

"I also should apologize for some slightly erroneous information after the first slide. Yes, human activity can cause an avalanche. Skiers have done so many times. As none of us ski I forgot all about it.

"Most of the time an avalanche happens when there are different types of snow layered on top of each other. Some types of snow will adhere to the previous snowfall but not always. The snow on the ground before this storm was wetter. The snow from this storm is dry. The two are not likely to stick together well and just about anything could set it off, including an animal.

"Brandon asked about setting off a controlled avalanche and under most circumstances that would be a good idea. However we can't rule out the possibility that the guys shooting arrows at us are in the danger zone. As we have a firm rule against taking a life unless it's absolutely necessary we can't take the chance."

"Is it likely that the avalanche could kill?" Cindy asked.

"I would classify it as a D2," Jeannie said. "It could injure or kill someone caught in it, particularly where these folks are hiding. The gully that gives them a spot to shoot from could also trap them."

"Thanks, Jeannie. Now I'd like Gavin to tell us what he told me this afternoon. He is also joining us on the council," Brandon said.

After repeating what he'd told Brandon Gavin continued. "I played around with it on all of our equipment. They work. I don't think they'd stop a bullet completely but they will stop an arrow."

"What would a bullet do?" Josh asked.

"It would probably be like wearing a bullet proof vest. You wouldn't be seriously hurt but it would cause a serious bruise. I don't know about you but I'm not sure I want to use something live to test the theory."

"We could use a pumpkin or something," Annette suggested.

"No need. I used a piece of two by four and it just left a bit of a dent, hence my thinking it would just be a bruise."

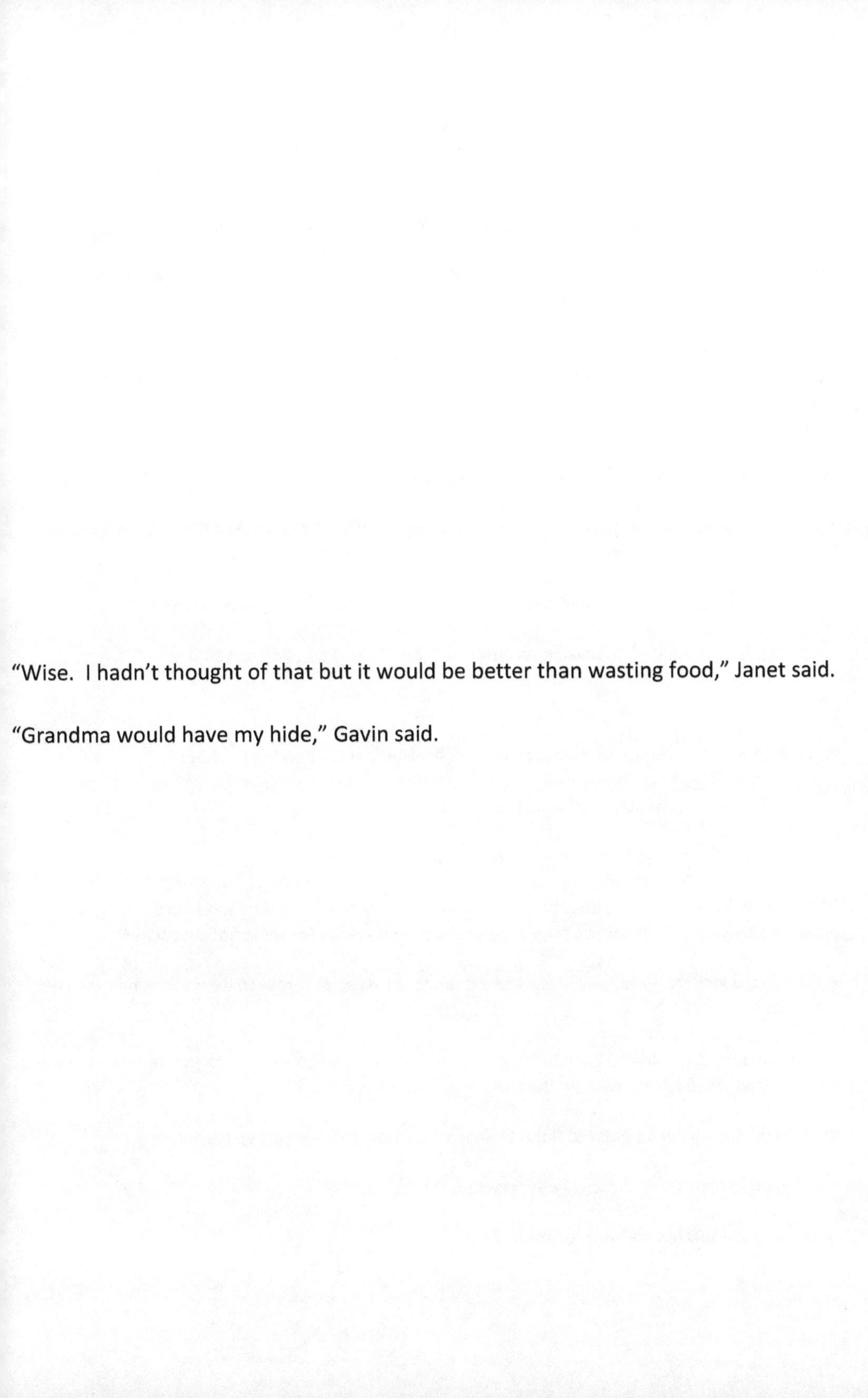

"Wise. I hadn't thought of that but it would be better than wasting food," Janet said.

"Grandma would have my hide," Gavin said.

Day Four

As predicted the storm passed by morning and it was a clear, sunny day.

"Today we are doing snow sculptures," Reilly announced at breakfast. "The area set aside is on the garden side of the houses. For the children there is snow in the empty barn so they don't get as cold."

"That will also keep them safe," Annette said. "Josh is going to be in charge of Petey and Mikey so we can work on dinner. He wants it backwards but he's not planning a contest for it this year. The time between the end of the contest and dinner is devoted to practice. Tomorrow is the first round of shows."

"I take it there will be six courses again?" Brandon asked.

"Yes, a lot of people told us they were glad it was a larger meal. They also liked the edible decorations. Before you start worrying I'm doing salad. It's fast, easy and I can do it sitting down."

"I'm going to do scampi and striped bass," Brandon said. "Does anyone else need pasta?"

"I do," Mr. Jamison said. "I'm making spaghetti and meatballs. I was hoping you'd offer."

"Not a problem."

When Brandon had finished his own preparations he went out to check on the boys.

"I see you made a snowman, Petey," he told the little boy.

"Mikey helped," Petey said. "He making a hover cart."

"It does look like a hover cart, doesn't it," Brandon said. The cart was a little lopsided but quite well done for a six-year-old. "I bet you guys win a prize. Are you ready for some hot chocolate?"

"I think all the kids are," Josh said. "Let's take them to the daycare center so we don't bother the chefs too much."

"I would imagine they already have the stuff we need ready," Brandon said. Annette had started putting it together when he left to check on the kids.

Once inside the boys were quick to finish their snack and join their age group playing.

"No sign of problems?" Brandon quietly asked Josh.

"None with the kids but we were all inside."

"I'll check with the sentries. I doubt we'll have any today unless they try to shoot the lights again."

Henry was on duty when Brandon went to the guard area in the trees.

"No sign of them," Henry said. "Do we know when the next storm is coming?"

"Day after tomorrow is the last I heard. I think tomorrow will be an inside day, though. It's supposed to be pretty windy."

"I wish we had a way to warn them of the danger they're in. I hate just waiting for the inevitable."

"I think we all do but how would we do it and would they listen if we tried?"

"Probably not."

After leaving the sentry post Brandon went to find Dr. Mike.

"How prepared are we for dealing with potential major injuries?" he asked.

"Dr. Cora brought me some supplies if we have to do major surgery. I'm just cautious about using them. Are you thinking about those folks with the arrows?"

"Yes, I am. There's no way to warn them and from what Jeannie said last night we're not going to have just one slide. It'll happen all winter."

"Do you think they'd go to the same area after an event of that nature?"

"I don't know how stubborn they are. We don't know much about them. None of us have the same training Grandma and Gary have."

"Well, I've been told what she did. She got a lot of information about the camps just from one arrow."

"Yeah, maybe Trevor and I should have a look. He learned a lot from his grandmother."

The two took the arrows into the council chambers to study them.

"My first question would be what did they use to color them," Trevor said. "The black is easy. It's charcoal. I'm guessing the white is kaolin."

"Next up would be what kind of metal they used. I brought a tool kit similar to what I saw Grandma use and a few of my own. Let's scrape the coloring off so we can see."

"For a group that doesn't believe in technology they certainly use some of it," Trevor said. "Alex's arrows are all iron. These look like an alloy. There's a lot of iron in it but it's sturdier, almost like steel."

"Steel? Where would they get steel?"

"I don't think it's that hard to do but it takes a lot more heat than iron and it's a longer process. James would know."

"Good point, let's ask him."

James looked at the arrows carefully.

"Yes, I'd say this is steel," he told them. "These are very carefully crafted. I could make arrows like them if we needed steel arrows. The tips I make are almost exactly like this."

"So this isn't something that could be made in a day," Brandon asked.

"No. The ore has to be dug up, the fire needs to be hot and the impurities have to be more or less cooked out of the ore. After that it was poured into a mold and then it was shaped by a blacksmith. Although he probably made a bunch of molds at a time it would take hours to make just one arrow and have it properly balanced like this is."

"So they have time to make things and enough people to have a dedicated expert to one thing," Brandon concluded.

"I would say they'd need two or more dedicated experts," James said. "Someone has to know how to mine the ore. I can do it, and usually I am the one who does it but our needs in the metal department were largely met by the folks who made the cryo program."

"I hadn't thought of that. To be able to fire these off and leave them must mean they have a quantity of them," Trevor said. "Something they don't regard as important enough to retrieve. I sure want my arrows back."

"I had wondered why they didn't seem to object to my shop," James said. "Since they have their own they must not see it as 'technology.' I wonder why they'd think a horse carriage was?"

"They probably work with wood but as they don't keep animals it could seem that way," Brandon said. "It's time for me to head back and finish up my part of dinner. Mikey and Petey are going to enjoy this."

When dessert was brought out first there were the usual startled gasps.

"Daddy, why are we having dessert first?" Mikey said as he ate his pumpkin soufflé.

"Because we are having a backwards dinner," Brandon told him.

"Can we do this every day?"

"No, dear," Annette said. "Once a year is quite enough."

When the meal was over Mikey was extravagant in praise. "That was the bestest dinner I ever had," he said.

"Oh, I though Christmas dinner and Thanksgiving dinner…" his father teased.

"No, this was the best. I like having dessert first."

"As we aren't going to be participating in the talent show, let's head on up to our rooms," Annette suggested. "For some reason I'm tired."

Day Five

"Ladies and gentlemen, before we have a last practice session for the talent contest we are going to play Simon Says," Reilly announced.

"I know how to play that game," Mikey said. "Do you think Petey does?"

"No, I think he's still a little young for that one," Annette said. "I'll take him along with Emma to the nursery."

Mikey and Brandon enjoyed the game. The ultimate winner was Leon much to his surprise.

"I haven't played games in years," he said. "I forgot how fun they could be."

"It is easy to forget how to have fun," Brandon agreed. "Are you taking part in the talent show?"

"No, I'm on guard duty now that the casts are off. I'm glad to be back in action again even if I do need physical therapy to get my bow arm working properly again."

"Annette and I are on the judging panel, so we aren't participating either. I think I'll join you guys on the sentry posts until time for lunch."

"Jeannie wasn't joking about that wind," Leon said when they stepped out. "I'm glad all of our activities are indoors today."

"I feel for those guys watching us. I kind of hope they aren't but Benton thinks they're pretty tenacious."

"Sometimes the term is downright bull-headed," Leon replied. "Which this is."

After lunch the first round of the talent contest began. There were several interesting acts but the two most memorable were Ally with Thi and Brin with Cindy.

"Ally has mastered all of the Waker weapons," Thi said proudly. "We will be doing a demonstration with the slingshot and the bow."

Those who didn't hunt were impressed with the prowess of the two young people, though they did not make it to the next round of competition.

"Brin will be telling a legend while I play background music on the recorder," Cindy said.

Brin wove a tale about a beautiful woman who was destined for great honor. Her father set a test for the young men who came to claim her hand but when the young men saw it they faltered. At last a young man came who liked the challenge. He succeeded and the couple was married.

As the show ended Leon came with an urgent message for Brandon.

"It's started. We need to send out a rescue team," the note read.

After showing the note to Annette Brandon began to tag people for the rescue.

"Abe, Trevor, Benton, Brin and Thi, come with me. Dr. Mike, head for the emergency treatment area and get ready for possible major injuries. Dr. Duff, go with him. Gavin, you come with us and drive. You know how to operate the force field. Let's go."

The avalanche had barely stopped when the team arrived. They could see one man had escaped and was running away without his bow or arrows.

"Use a suit blower to unbury him," Trevor told Brin. "I can see his head and his left arm. It's seriously broken."

Before long the blower had the man unburied and Brandon began to prepare him to be moved. "His leg is pretty messed up as well. I don't know about neck or back injuries, so let's use a brace and backboard," he told Trevor.

"He's lucky to be alive," Benton said. "Perhaps we will learn more about them as he recovers."

"If he recovers," Thi said, his face slightly green at the sight of the injuries.

"The Wakers have great medicine," Benton said. "If he can be saved he will be."

As quickly as it was safe to do they loaded the man into the hover cart and took off for the hospital part of the complex.

"What do we have," Dr. Mike said as they carried him in.

"I don't know about other injuries but his arm and his leg are going to need surgery," Brandon said. "You said you got some stuff we might need from Dr. Cora, would that include actual surgical stuff?"

"It would. I want you and Trevor to scrub. Trevor you can hand me things. Brandon, you can monitor his vitals and handle the anesthesia. Dr. Duff, you and I are going to repair his arm and leg. There is no obvious misalignment with the neck or spine though we can't rule out injuries there. Getting the bleeding stopped in his obvious injuries is going to have to take priority."

It took four hours to repair the damage done by the sliding snow. The man moaned slightly as he was moved into a hospital bed but didn't wake up.

"Do you think he's going to make it?" Trevor asked Dr. Mike.

"I think so. We'll have to watch for signs of internal bleeding and infections. He's going to have a rough time for a while and I don't know if he's going to understand what happened."

"If they don't like technology is he going to appreciate the pins and stuff?"

"He isn't going to be in much of a position to do anything about it. Hopefully by the time he is he'll understand."

"I hope so. I'm beat and I didn't even operate."

"You did good, kid."

Dr. Mike gave the report on the patient at the council meeting that evening.

"He has awakened slightly but he's much too ill to talk much less answer questions. It will be a while before we get any information from him."

"We can still get information about him," Brandon said. "Trevor is bringing some of his belongings for us to examine. Grandma taught him a great deal and I've picked up some from her as well. Anyone else with information can chime in."

Trevor came in carrying a hat, scarf, gloves, socks, boots and a knife.

"They knit and they crochet," Henrietta said. "The socks were knitted and the scarf is crocheted." She examined the two items more closely. "The materials are wool, cotton and flax. There isn't as much wool as plant material so they either gather what they find when the animals shed or perhaps use what's on an animal hide after the hunters bring it in.

"The hat is sheep's fur, so they process furs and leather. The gloves are some other type of leather, probably cow and I suspect the boots are but it's hard to tell with the dye."

"What kind of dye did they use?" Brandon asked.

"My guess would be red ochre," Henrietta replied.

"The boots have nails, made similarly to the arrows we already looked at," James said. "The knife is also metal with a bone handle. It's steel and quite sharp."

"So while they don't have technology as advanced as ours they do use machines of some sort," Brandon said. "I would consider a spinning wheel and a loom a machine."

"From the craftsmanship I would guess they have industries something like we do," Henrietta said. "It takes time to produce the kind of leather in the boots and gloves. It also takes time to make them.

"Unless someone is going to be out in the cold for a prolonged period of time we mostly use knitted or crocheted gloves, particularly for the kids. They lose them too fast to waste the time and the other resources it would take to make something like this."

"Our winter clothing is similar but we had not thought of nailing thick hides to the bottom of our shoes," Benton said. "We rely on many layers and avoid spending a lot of time outside in the winter."

"None of these items are similar to anything we make," Brin said. "The women do weave but they do not make things like the socks and scarf."

"Do you go out much in winter?" Abe asked.

"No, unless we run out of meat and then it is dangerous. Some hunters don't come back," Brin said. "It is one of the many reasons the Camps are so grateful to the Wakers. Many deaths have been prevented and I am glad to call myself a Waker now."

"I have a question," Amaya said. "After this next storm wouldn't it be wise to find where these people are camping?"

"We don't need to wait until the storm is over," Trevor said. "The board suits have heaters and during a snowstorm is probably the best time for us to spy on our spies."

"What would we gain by doing that?" Mr. Richards asked. "I find the anthropology being done fascinating but what would be the purpose?"

"The more we know about them the better we will be able to deal with them," Brandon said. "If we know what makes them do the things they are doing we can find a way to work around them so as to avoid all-out war, which they would not win."

"How do you know they wouldn't win?"

"We have superior weapons, we can call in more people and we can travel faster than they can over terrain and in conditions they can't travel in," Abe replied. "We don't believe in using that superiority unless we have to. The more we know the less likely it will be that we have to fight them."

"They are not lovers of peace," Benton warned.

"I think it will depend greatly on their culture and what we learn about it. Until we met them the Camps and the Caves did not get along," Brandon replied.

"If any people can do it the Wakers can," Benton said. "Now who are we going to send?"

"I want to go," Trevor said.

"I'd like to but with three kids and one on the way I'd better not," Brandon said. "Unmarried folks only."

"I'll go with him," Henry said. "Until we know their views on women we might want to keep it men only. I don't want to put anyone in harm's way unnecessarily."

"If I knew how to fly one of those boards I'd go," Amaya said. "I can choose to take a risk."

"I'll teach you," Trevor said. "If we thought that a woman would be better able to talk to them, and who knows? It might be so, it would be better if only women went. It's just a way of preventing trouble."

"I understand but I still say I'd prefer to make my own choice, thanks," Amaya said.

"Ok, we have a team," Brandon broke in. "When do you want to go?"

"Now is as good a time as any," Trevor said. "It's already snowing and there's enough wind to make it harder for them to notice any movement we might make."

The wind wasn't howling but it did blow the snow around making it harder to see. The two rode the hover boards for about ten miles before finding the camp. It was tucked into a hollow with sheer sides.

"I see ten tents," Trevor told Henry over the suit radio. "One of them is bigger than the others; let's see if we can get a little closer."

"Ok, I can hear them now, can you?" Henry asked as they landed behind a rock.

"Loud and clear. It seems they're discussing the avalanche," Trevor said.

"Did they cause it to fall?" a man's voice asked.

"No, not that I could see. They did come out after it fell. If I had been able to find my bow I would have shot the thing they were in."

"What if these are the Later People?" a younger voice asked. "They have not hurt us even though we have shot at them."

"I am afraid of those machines they use," an elderly voice said. "It is not natural."

"Not everything we do is natural," the first man said. "What Jai has said is something to consider."

"Do you believe in the Later People?" the spy asked.

"Yes, I do. There have been rumors for several years that a people who use a great deal of Technology are walking among us. I suggest caution."

"I suggest we keep watching," the spy said. "Though not near where the river of snow ran. Who knows if it will happen again?"

"What about shooting at their machines?" the elderly voice said. "If it is the Later People we will not hurt them. If it is not what they are doing is forbidden."

"I think it is safe to continue shooting machines. As you say, if it is the Later People no one would be harmed," the man's voice said.

"I am willing to go," the spy said.

"Who will you take with you? Kalel is no longer with us."

"I will take Jai. He has reached manhood. Perhaps we will find out if Kalel is still alive, though I could not see him in the snow."

"I've heard enough," Henry told Trevor. "Let's go report."

When they re-entered the council chamber coffee and sandwiches were waiting. Trevor gratefully took a huge bite.

"They're going to continue to spy on us," Henry said after repeating the belief in a Later People. "They believe that if we are these Later People we won't be hurt if they shoot at our machines. I think we'd better stick to hover carts and boards until we can make some kind of meaningful contact."

"Were there any women at the meeting?" Annette asked.

"No, there weren't. We can tentatively infer that they aren't part of the decision making process but it doesn't tell us if they are totally misogynistic," Henry said.

"It took us a long time to accept that women could and should do everything a man does," Brin said. "It may well be the same for them."

"Does that mean it's safe for us to do stuff outside?" Reilly asked.

"As long as it doesn't involve animals or machines," Brandon replied. "Why?"

"The scavenger hunt is tomorrow, followed by round two of the competitions."

"We better get a good night's sleep then," Annette said. "Petey is going to want to take part."

"I'll carry him. He'll have to put up with it or he can stay with the younger kids," Brandon said.

Day Six

"Ladies and gentlemen, this morning we are to have our scavenger hunt. Those who have tasks involved with this may assume your stations. The rest of you can either go in groups or singly. Please come and receive your list of items to find."

"Would you like to show me how this is done?" Brin asked Cindy. "I'm afraid I don't know what he's talking about."

"We're going to get a list of things to find. We'll be going all over the place, though both of us know where some things are likely to be. Reilly promised there would be surprises, though. Let's get our list."

After collecting the list of twenty-five items Brin asked Cindy, "What was life like for you before this cryo sleep?"

"It was different. I spent most of my time growing up in a big city. There was very little grass and few trees unless we went to a park. It was fun but I was really rebellious. I didn't want to do what my parents told me to do and I got into trouble at school. Finally they sent me to live with my grandparents."

"Did they teach you?"

"They did, but probably not the way you were taught. They lived in a forest and there wasn't a lot to do, at least not the things I was used to doing. It was quiet, something a city never is. I learned to like that and to enjoy walking in the woods.

"My grandmother taught me how to help in her garden, which is why I spend most of my time doing that. They didn't keep animals so while I help Amaya she's had to teach me.

"I especially liked her flower gardens."

"What were the flowers for?"

"They probably had uses but she didn't grow them for any purpose other than looking nice. She had a lot of roses, some scented geraniums and snapdragons. There were a lot of others but those are the ones I remember best."

"Roses I have seen but I have no idea what the other two are."

"I haven't seen either of them around but I haven't really been looking. I don't go on the hunting or foraging missions so I don't know what's out there."

2090 Tech No New Year's Day

"I know you told us not to be seen working the animals but I have got to walk a horse," Cindy told Brandon. "She's showing early signs of colic and I want to stop it."

"Take someone with you. I don't think Amaya can help with her arm still in a cast."

"Brin can help. It might be wise to have Amaya there because he is kind of afraid of the horses."

"Go ahead, but be careful."

"If you must walk this horse then of course I will come," Brin said. "Amaya can keep the radio. If there are problems we can deal with them."

"This horse is going to want to roll, so stay clear of her unless I need help getting her up," Cindy said.

The horse wasn't quite that bad off though she did balk at walking.

"Come on, girl," Cindy said, gently tugging the lead rope. "You need to... OUCH!"

This spooked the horse who decided running would be a good idea. Amaya chased her and brought her back while Brin examined the arrow in Cindy's leg.

"These people have no respect," he spat. "No warrior would shoot a woman without good cause."

"I've radioed Brandon. They said leave the arrow alone. Brin, you need to keep walking the horse. She's better but she won't make it if she doesn't keep walking."

"I will care for her. You care for Cindy. When I find these miscreants I will bring them before our council."

"Glad you aren't going after them yourself," Cindy said in a weak voice.

"Wakers don't kill unless we have to," Brin said with dignity as he walked the horse. "We also don't shoot people for no reason."

Brandon, Abe and Dr. Duff arrived quickly. Brandon was a little surprised to see Brin calmly walking the horse but then turned his attention to Cindy.

"I think Dr. Duff and I can handle this," Brandon said. "Abe, I'd like to know where the shooter was and if possible where he went. Amaya, is the horse well enough to go back in her stall?"

"I think so, but I'll withhold food and water for a few more hours," Amaya said.

"Brin, you go with Abe. When you get back we'll give you an update on Cindy and discuss what to do next."

"Do you know how to ride a hover board?" Abe asked.

"Yes, Trevor taught me. What are we to do when we find this person?"

"We listen quietly. We need more information about them."

It didn't take long and the conversation was loud enough that the two searchers didn't have to get close.

"...told only to fire at machines! That wasn't a machine. It was a person."

"She was leading an animal. Those animals get attached to machines. What is the difference?"

"The difference is that we are not to shoot people, not even women. You have much to learn, Jai."

"It does prove they are people."

"That doesn't get you out of trouble. You will have extra duty tonight."

"Yes, sir."

The voices were moving away at that point. Abe looked at Brin after they were out of earshot.

"So we're people, are we?"

"Yes and they seem to have a negative view of women. It is good that none are in harm's way, though I doubt that will stop them."

"No, but arrows will."

"Yes, I wish to find out how Cindy is doing. I am glad that the person who shot her will be punished."

"I'm glad you didn't do it yourself. I get the feeling that you care for her."

"I do. At home I would ask my grandfather if I might court her. Who do I ask here?"

"You might try asking her. After that talk to Brandon."

Abe and Brin reported the conversation to the council.

"So they are to shoot at our machines but they aren't supposed to shoot people," Brandon said. "I'm glad they at least think we are people."

"They are not respecters of women," Brin said. "I used to feel that way but I have learned. I wonder if they are capable of learning."

"It's hard to say, Brin. Perhaps not all of them feel that way. We've had men who wouldn't take orders from women, at least not at first. Most of them learned, some are still serving time in jail, though that is the least of their infractions," Brandon replied.

"Are we still planning on having a New Year's ball?" Amaya asked. "People are pretty upset about Cindy."

"Yes, we will," Annette replied. "Her injury wasn't as severe as Trevor's. If she's careful she could probably attend though dancing is not something she should do."

"I will sit with her," Brin said.

Everyone cheered when Cindy hobbled into the common room on crutches.

"Why is everyone cheering?" she asked Brin.

"Because we have all been worrying about you," Brin said. "If you have no objections I will sit with you while the others dance."

"That would be wonderful. Brandon was pretty emphatic about me staying off my leg for a few days."

"You are a brave woman. The women of the Camps would not be willing to leave their fire for many days after something like this. They would be too afraid."

"Brandon told me what you heard. I'm glad that the person who shot me will be punished somehow. I don't think we've seen the last of their arrows, though."

"Why do you think that?"

"They have yet to see the hover carts and hover boards. If they plan to shoot at machines those will be fired on."

"That is true. I am glad there is a form of protection for them though I'm not certain what it is."

"It's not something you can see; it's a type of magnetic field. You've seen the magnets that James uses and that the children use in school, right?"

"Yes. I've seen stones like that as well. They are very valuable."

"They would be. Those are called magnets and the shields use a similar idea. Something thrown at the craft will bounce off the shield rather than hit the craft or the people in it."

"That makes more sense. I know that when two like ends of these magnets are aimed at each other they are repelled."

"Exactly."

"I hope you and I are more like the ends that join together."

"You do?"

"Yes. Abe told me I should address you first. Is that a normal thing for Wakers?"

"Yes, it is. And I believe we are very much like the ends of the magnet that join together."

"Are there other customs?"

"As my father didn't survive the plague you can't ask him but you can ask Brandon."

"That is also what Abe said. Abe is a wise man."

"Yes, he is. Oh, look! Trevor and Amaya are dancing."

"Yes, I believe they have a similar attachment. Thi and Ally as well. I think Brandon will be busy."

"I do believe so although he may bring Grandma and Grandpa down to perform the ceremonies. That would be very nice."

"I would like that. I have as much respect for Grandpa and Grandma as I do for Neram."

While Brin and Cindy were talking a runner brought a note to Brandon.

"Abe, can you come with me?" Brandon asked. "Kalel, our wounded guest, is awake enough to talk a little bit."

"Certainly. He may want to know what the others think happened to him and I want to know more about their myth."

"I figured you would. I'd ask for Brin and/or Trevor but they seem to be rather… occupied."

Abe smiled. "Yes. I am proud of Brin. He's in love with Cindy and he didn't take out the spies. Instead he followed instructions. He's going to ask to talk to you soon, I think."

"I'm expecting more than just that pair," Brandon said. "Let's find out if we are the Later People."

Kalel was propped up and slowly sipping a cup of broth.

"How are you feeling?" Brandon asked. "Do you need something for pain?"

"The other man gave me something a few minutes ago. Where am I and what have you done to my arm and leg?"

"You are in our hospital," Brandon said. "You were hit by an avalanche. Your fellow spy called it a river of snow, and it is that in a way. The avalanche broke your arm and your leg. We had to do surgery to repair the damage. There are pins and plates holding the bones in place so they may heal. When they're healed we will take the outside pieces off but we'll probably leave the inside pieces in place."

"Are you the Later People?"

"When our searchers found your campsite they heard mention of the Later People but we have no idea what that means."

"The Later People will teach us how to safely and wisely use machinery to make our lives better. Until then we are not allowed."

"We are allowed. It is how we were able to save your life. As for being the Later People, it's possible; I'd have to know a lot more. The last group of people who thought we were the fulfillment of their religion thought we were deities... and we aren't.

"For now, though, you need to get more rest. There will be someone available around the clock if you need anything."

"Thank you."

Day Eight the Story of the Later People

"Brandon, Amaya wants to learn how to ride a hover board. If we do it in the empty barn would that be ok?" Trevor asked.

"Yes, it should be harder for them to shoot you in a barn. However I don't trust them so make sure you use the force fields."

After carefully taking the boards into the barn Trevor began to show Amaya how they worked.

"They're really easy to ride. They have a homing beacon so you can get back to wherever base is even if you get lost or it's dark. The steering is a lot like a bicycle or motorcycle. The brakes are on the handlebars.

"The most important button we have under these circumstances is this one in the corner. When you press it the force field comes on. See if you can touch my arm."

"No, I can't. I can't even get within four inches of it. That's amazing."

"Yes, it is. Even though we're in a barn we need to leave the doors open for light and ventilation. That's been added but not hooked up until we have animals to put in here. It is possible to shoot through the open door."

"So we use the force fields."

"Absolutely."

After about an hour Amaya was adept on the board.

"Hey, this is fun," she said.

"I've always thought so even when I've had to use them in scary situations."

"What was tha…"

An arrow bounced off the force field of Amaya's board. The impact startled her and she fell off.

"Are you ok?" Trevor asked, helping her sit up.

"Yeah, I'm fine. I don't think I would be without that force field, though. Let's leave the boards here and report to Brandon."

"Let's report to Brandon and wait until they give us an all clear," Trevor said. "I don't need scared like that again soon."

Brandon took the report and then called Nelson.

"I want you to see if you can find where these guys are hiding now," he said. "This is beginning to make me angry."

"Should I tranq them and bring them in?"

"Not yet. Kalel should be able to talk more today and he can give us more information. We'll need a plan."

It didn't take Nelson long to find the hiding spot. It had a perfect view of the barn doors. He could also hear slight sounds of people talking, so he followed them.

"They are the Later People," Jai said. "That arrow should have hit that machine."

"That arrow was aimed a little high for hitting a machine, Jai. You aimed at the girl."

"So? She's a girl and it wouldn't have mattered."

"Yes, it would. Girls become women. Women become mothers. Unless you can give birth you would be killing off part of the next generation. Your views on this are not in line with what you were taught.

"As for them being the Later People, I agree. She was unharmed and the arrow fell away long before it could hit anything. It is like they have a wall in the air. We must report this and you are in for extra duty again."

"Yes, sir."

Nelson quietly turned his board and headed back.

"So they aren't all that misogynistic," Brandon said. "Apparently women have at least some value. How much we'll have to find out, maybe from Kalel. I almost wish Dr. Cora was here. I'd have her go in to tend him and see how he handled it."

"He's polite to Merideth when she comes in to check on him," Nelson said. "Though that may be because of this Later People thing."

"I'll go and talk to him again. If he's up to it I'll get more information."

When Brandon went into Kalel's hospital room the man was awake.

"Are the pain medications working?" he asked.

"Yes, but they make me sleepy. Are they supposed to do that?"

"It is how they work. There are pain medications that don't make people sleepy but they wouldn't be strong enough for the pain you are likely to feel. We have learned that it is important to stay ahead of the pain because once it gets bad it is very hard to get it under control again."

"You really are the Later People."

"I'd like to know more about that, actually. What are the Later People?"

"In the beginning of our people a man woke up. Our people were outside of a strange building and trying to open the doors. The man said that we were not to open the doors nor use the Technology inside. There would be people who would come later to open the doors and teach us how to use Technology.

"Since then we have not used any machinery that we did not already have. Using Technology is a crime punishable by death. We have not seen much of this until you came. We have heard rumors that there are people who use Technology but they are far to the north of us."

"Do you know where this building is?"

"Yes, we guard it carefully."

"Good. Now our spies have heard some comments about women. How does your society treat them?"

"They are not usually as important as the men. There have been exceptions. It is expected that the Later People will explain many things to us and perhaps this is one of them. The woman who tends me seems to be an equal."

"All of our women are equals. My wife and I are co-leaders."

"I have often thought that is how it should be. When I wed my wife will be my equal."

"How do I get your people to stop shooting arrows at us and our machinery?"

"You will have to let them know who you are. There will be many changes and you will have to teach us. I don't know how you will do that but it is said that you can get from place to place faster than our fastest runner."

"That is true; however we spend a great deal of our time during the warmer seasons preparing for winter. We will go on a mission in the spring, before planting starts but I will have to get help from the other communities if we are to visit all of your people."

"So it is true. There are others of you north of us."

"Yes. We are known as the Wakers by most people. We wake up the people still sleeping in the cryo cases."

"That is another fulfillment. We were told they must be left alone until you came."

"Yeah, most of the people who woke up early from cryo sleep were told that. It has made for all kinds of problems but they're solved now."

"That is good. When may I return to my people?"

"It will be several weeks. The bones in your arm and leg were shattered. It will take time for that to heal."

"Why did you not cut them off?"

"We don't need to do that. It's much better for you to keep them if they can be repaired."

"I am glad. It would be impossible to do much if I lost both limbs."

"You will hunt again if that reassures you. Some of the other peoples need to hear that."

"Yes, I have heard of them though I've seen few of them. I am a hunter but I am also a leatherworker. I could get by just doing that but it would be difficult with only one arm."

"Having worked with hides myself I can understand that. Now you should rest more."

"Yes, the medicine is making me sleepy again."

Trevor insisted both on accompanying Amaya to the council meeting and on staying to hear what was going on.

"I was going to add you to the council anyway," Brandon said. After repeating what Kalel had said and hearing Nelson's report Benton spoke up.

"I wish to speak with him. I may not get much more information but I am curious if he is aware of the Caves."

"I would also like to speak to him," Brin said. "You say he knows of the phrase "I will hunt again." That indicates that it isn't as important to him."

"I would gather not. He said that he hunted but he didn't have to. He could just be a leatherworker," Brandon said. "We have specialists who rarely, if ever, hunt."

"This is true. I would like to know where he heard it."

"It might give us more insight to how they think," Cindy said.

"Is he likely to be awake?" Benton asked.

"It's been a few hours since his last pain pill so it's possible," Brandon said. "Just don't stay long."

Benton went in to see Kalel first. The man was trying to eat a sandwich one handed.

"We have met your people before," Benton said. "It has been many years."

"You are the people of many metals," Kalel said. "I was a child but my people were astounded. I have even seen the arrows."

"The Caves do use many metals," Benton replied. "I have seen your arrows prior to the ones that have been shot at us. We Wakers have many things the Caves do not but they are learning."

"You have joined the Wakers?"

"My family and I have. We are helping to bring all of the communities closer together. It is not just better for survival it helps us thrive."

"It is amazing. I know how fierce and loyal the Caves are. The Wakers seem to have done much."

"They have. Brin, formerly of the Camps would like to speak with you."

Kalel nodded and Brin came in as Benton exited.

"Are you a warrior?" Brin asked.

"I am when I must be," Kalel replied. "Usually I am a hunter and a leatherworker."

"Don't your women work the leather?"

"Some do. Some have other talents. They are often good hunters."

"I am glad you allow your women to hunt. Until the Camps met the Wakers ours were not."

"You are the people of the wooden arrows."

"No, I am a Waker now. The Camps are learning to use the weapons of the Wakers as they are more efficient for hunting."

"How did you become a Waker?"

"Three of us decided to join this community. My grandfather, the leader of all of the Camps, agreed."

"I have heard of your grandfather. His name is Neram, correct?"

"It is."

"You were to be the next leader."

"It is better for my people that I am here. I am a Waker now."

Day Ten Back to the Celebration

"You've missed a lot of the activities," Annette mentioned to her husband the next morning. "Are you going to have to do the same today?"

"I doubt it, though there will probably be a surreptitious look for more spies. I suspect they are on their way home with news that they have found the Later People."

"Mikey and Petey will be glad. Let's see what Reilly has planned for us today."

The Lord of Misrule stood and waited for silence.

"Today we will be having races. The snow has been blown off a suitable track area. If you do not wish to or can't participate there is a viewing stand."

"I would be in the 'can't participate' crowd, I know," Annette said before Brandon could say anything. "I wonder if Petey is old enough for races."

"I don't think so but I bet Josh has something planned. He's gotten pretty good at this."

When Reilly had finished Josh stood up.

"All children four and under are invited to remain here and do crafts with us," he said. "Parents if you have older children who you think are too young or may not be able to handle the cold, let us know. They are welcome to stay as well."

"That's good. Janet's younger son has a cold," Annette said. "By the way, the talent show has been set and will probably be on Twelfth Night."

"That's good. Hm. Trevor is making a bee-line for me. I'll meet you on the field."

"May I talk to you privately?" Trevor asked. He looked nervous.

"Yes, would you like to step into my office?"

"Yes, please." The young man turned red. "Amaya and I want to get married. Her father died in the plague so you're as close as I can come to asking someone."

"I'm not overly surprised," Brandon said. "Nor am I going to make comments about your age. I approve and I'm planning on calling for Grandma and Grandpa. I think there will actually be three weddings."

"Ally and Thi I know. Brin and Cindy?"

"Yes and yes. Let's head for the races, though I may be waylaid again before I get there."

The two headed for the tracks set up. Brandon almost made it to the front door before Thi caught him and Brin wasn't far behind. Figuring he'd better give Grandma and Grandpa as much time as possible he stopped by the radio room before going to the race track.

"Three weddings and one is our grandson? Of course we're coming," Grandpa said. "I'll let JoAn and Scot know. They'll want to be there as well."

"If the kids have their way it will be on Twelfth Night, which is day after tomorrow. Is that too soon?"

"It will be cutting it a little tight but I'm sure we can get there and help with the preparations. You know Grandma will want to be involved."

"Yeah, I know. I would imagine JoAn might also. Would you let Neram know? I'm not sure if he could manage the trip. Also, make sure everyone uses the force fields. Those new folks around us only just stopped shooting at us. I'll give you particulars when you get here."

"That sounds interesting. We will do that and keep our eyes out, Home Base out."

When Brandon finally made it to the field Mikey was about to run his first race. He grinned to see both of his parents watching him.

"You did great, Mikey," Brandon said. "You came in second. That was a good run."

"It was fun. Are you going to race?"

"I would imagine when they get around to people my age. Do you want to sit with mommy? I need to find Reilly and Henrietta."

Annette raised her eyebrows.

"I had a talk with Trevor, Thi, Brin and Grandpa. Tell you about it later but I'm pretty sure you can guess what's up."

"Yes, I can. They're a lot more obvious than they think they are. Are Grandpa and Grandma coming?"

"Wild horses couldn't keep them away though I did warn them about wild arrows."

Henrietta had been sitting with James watching the races. Four year old Myra had already competed and was enjoying a cuddle with her mother.

"Are you up for three weddings in two days?" Brandon asked.

Henrietta was unperturbed. "I've been preparing for it for the last month. They need to be fitted but their outfits are nearly done as are the decorations."

"How did you know?"

"Probably the same way most of us knew. Are Grandma and Grandpa coming?"

"Yes and most likely JoAn and Scot. Neram may also attend if he's well enough."

"It shouldn't be too arduous a journey by hover cart unless those Later People group are around."

"I've warned them. I don't think there will be a problem right at the moment but they will be keeping their shields up. We now know they work against those arrows."

"Even if it did shake Amaya and Trevor up. I suspect that the incident is what has prompted Trevor to speak up."

"As with Brin and Cindy when she got shot. Her leg is healing nicely so she should be able to walk down the aisle without a limp."

"I'm glad Amaya's arm is out of the cast. It would have made fitting her dress harder."

Reilly called Trevor over for a race at that point. James had decided to sit out the races.

After all of the races had been run, with Trevor and Jax winning in their division, Brandon went to find Nelson.

"Any sign of them?" Brandon asked.

"No, and I think we'd have had one if they'd seen us using the suit packs to blow the snow away from this area. We've checked all the likely spots and it's all clear."

"That's good. It will make it easier for Grandma and Grandpa when they get here."

"Why are they coming?"

"Three weddings, one involving their grandson," Brandon grinned.

"It's about time. All six of them have had their minds elsewhere."

"Neram may also choose to come."

"It would be appropriate as would Billy and Mirin. JoAn and Scot are coming as well, right?"

"Yes, which means we need to get cracking. Henrietta's been busy. I'm kind of hoping James has as well. Six rings take time."

"Not to mention an appropriate feast, celebrating the end of the holiday and the weddings."

"Yep, I'll be spending time in the kitchen."

⁂

Day Eleven Grandma and Grandpa arrive

"It looks like you brought an entire entourage," Annette said, hugging Grandma.

"A lot of people wanted to come," Grandma replied. "That baby is active."

"Tell me about it. It kicks Brandon awake sometimes."

"The girls did that to Grandpa. I think it's so they get a small taste of what it's like."

"So who all did come?"

"Neram, Billy, Mirin, Scot, JoAn, Noah and Tony. The latter two brought all kinds of goodies for the feast and of course we all brought wedding presents."

"Is Mirin expecting again?"

"Yes and I suspect JoAn is as well. Andrea wanted to come but as she is also in an expectant state it got vetoed."

"I suspect that Henrietta and Merideth are as well. We could have a lot of interesting announcements soon."

"Look, Brin is introducing Cindy to Neram," Brandon said as he came up to the two women. "He seems to like her."

"She's hard not to like. She's a hard worker and hasn't complained about her leg even though it's still got to hurt," Annette said.

"I think Brin is telling Neram that story now. He looks bone tired. We ought to get him inside where he can sit down."

"Yes, I think we could all use a hot drink and a snack. Then the kitchen staff needs to sit down with us and discuss food," Grandma said.

"I'd like to talk to some of the council about this arrow business," Grandpa said. "Could we do that?"

"Yes, I'll get Abe, Nelson, Henry and Benton. There are others who could be useful but they are..."

"Yes, they'll be busy the next two days at least. I can get an overview with the five of you."

After being told of what happened, Grandpa went to visit Kalel.

"Kalel, this is Grandpa. He is one of the senior leaders of the Wakers," Brandon said by way of introduction.

"Grandpa is a suitable name. You are one of the elders?"

"You could say that," Grandpa said. "Grandma and I were the first two of our communities to wake up."

"I have already decided you are the Later People. Will you tell my people and help us as was promised in the beginning?"

"We will. It has not yet been decided who will go but we will do so when winter is over. Even with our technology it is wiser not to spend too much time outdoors when it is cold and snowing."

"Agreed. I am glad. I'm glad that my life was saved and so were my arm and my leg. My people would not have been able to fix them."

"We have a fine medical team," Grandpa said. "Many lives have been saved and we will continue to do so."

"Time for you to rest more," Brandon said as he came into the room. "Merideth said it's time for you to take these."

"How long before I may try the medications that don't cause me to sleep?"

"Probably not until we take the pins out."

Kalel sighed.

Brandon led Grandpa to his office where he poured both of them a glass of wine.

"To Trevor and the rest of our engaged couples," he said by way of a toast.

"Here, here."

"We're going to need help with a mission the size Kalel is talking about," Brandon said after taking a sip.

"You'll get it. This is a golden opportunity to unite more of the people."

"I wonder what kind of technology is hidden away and so carefully guarded?"

"I'm afraid you won't be able to be on that mission. Not when you'll have four kids."

Brandon sighed. "I know and I don't regret it. After the festivities tomorrow we'll have a council meeting so we can all discuss it. I'd like you, Grandma and Neram to sit in on it and help us plan. I'm pretty sure we're going to need some people that aren't living here to go along."

"I'm not so sure. As long as we can get you help prepping for next winter I think you have the makings of a good team already here."

"If you say so. You know a lot more about this than I do. Let's go find out what everyone else is up to."

While Brandon was talking with Grandpa several other important conversations were going on.

"Are you ready for your fittings?" Henrietta asked the three brides.

"You mean you already have gowns for us?" Amaya asked.

"I do. I already know your sizes as I've made clothing for you before. I just need to do a final fitting."

"These are gorgeous," Cindy said. "Why is Ally's blue?"

"Our customs are that the bride wears white. The customs of the Camps are that they are the colors of the earth. As another custom of ours involves a poem and because the color becomes her I chose blue."

"What does the poem say about white and blue?" Amaya asked.

"Marry in white, you've chosen right. Marry in blue, your love is true."

"Are there colors you don't get married in?" Ally asked.

"Yes, red and black have negative meanings. Now, turn around. Yes, these fit. Here are the veils, also set up to go with your gown. You will be beautiful brides."

"I think so too," Amaya said. "However as another custom is that the grooms don't get to see us in our gowns until the wedding we'd better change. I'm betting all you have to do is fit them as well?"

"Quite true on both counts."

Meanwhile Grandma was in her favorite room of any house; the kitchen. Noah was already busy working on cakes and other desserts and Tony was fussing with pasta and sauces.

"It's nice to have someone that really knows desserts working on this," Annette said. "What are you going to make?"

"My usual things. Trevor wants trout pate and Amaya wants my soup. Brandon is handling the seafood, right?"

"Yes and probably glad he's not handling the pasta. He's got a lot on his plate."

"You both do. I am glad to see you're not overdoing. Sometimes first time mothers don't know when to stop."

"I've had three good examples of why I should pay attention. Heather, Mirin and Dr. Cora."

"Well, Mirin didn't overdo but she did have high blood pressure and wound up on bed rest because of it."

"Is that why Brandon checks my blood pressure every day?"

"Does he?" Grandma looked amused. "Probably and it isn't a bad idea."

"Why are you smiling?"

"Because he's doing precisely what Alderson did and what Grandpa would have done if he'd known how to take blood pressure. He's nervous."

"I suspect with good cause. We don't have an O.B. down here."

"Dr. Mike has assured me he's done quite a few C-Sections should that be needed and the other doctors seem to be aware of what may or may not need done."

"Good because I'm not the only pregnant lady anymore."

"We're doing what the cryo team wanted; reseeding the planet."

Day Twelve Weddings, Festivities and a Council Meeting

"Myra looks so cute," Amaya said with a nervous giggle.

"So does Mikey and I love that serious expression," Cindy said.

"He doesn't want to mess up," Ally said. "He was asking Brandon about it a few minutes ago."

"They'll both do just fine. Oh, good! Somebody brought Kalel in to watch," Amaya said.

"That's our cue," Cindy said as the procession started down the aisle.

After the ceremony they went into the dining hall for the feast. Not only was it for the wedding it was also the end of Twelfth Night.

"I'm glad Grandma came," Trevor said as he enjoyed his pate. "I'm going to have to learn how to make this."

"I'm glad Tony came," Brandon said. "All I had to do was make the clams."

"With all the chefs I didn't even have to make the salad," Annette said.

When dessert was brought out everyone stood up and clapped. Besides three wedding cakes there were a number of Noah's chocolate creations.

Reilly stood up. "Ladies and gentlemen, this is the last night of our celebration. As a finale we are going to have a talent show made up of several acts that were judged to be the best in their class."

Some of the acts were funny. Others, like Brin and Cindy's were spooky. He told the story of a ghost that would walk out of a thick mist and scare passersby. Finally Abe and Jax came on stage. Jax carried a guitar and an expectant hush fell over the audience.

"While we usually stick to John Denver music we thought we'd start with a little Simon and Garfunkle," Abe said. Their first song was Sound of Silence followed by Scarborough Fair.

"Now this last song everybody has to sing. By now you all know it." Jax played the opening chords to Country Roads and the crowd sang. Needless to say they were voted the best act of the evening.

After the crowd broke up those Brandon had tagged for the council meeting headed for the chamber. Extra chairs were brought in so that Neram, Grandma and Grandpa had seats.

"Has everyone been brought up to speed on the situation?" Brandon asked.

"Yes, Grandpa told Neram and me about it," Grandma said.

"We need to mount a mission starting as early as possible this spring," Brandon said. "The mission will be to talk to the various clans of this group. For lack of a better term I'm going to call them the Later People group even though we're supposedly the Later People.

"Another important part of this mission is to find the building they've been guarding, open it up and find out what's inside. I'm just hoping whatever it is will be useful and not dangerous."

"It would be a safe bet that it's useful. As for dangerous anything can be used the wrong way," Grandma said. "Who do you plan on sending?"

"That is up for debate first. Much as I'd love to go I can't. By the time the expedition heads out I'll have four children or very nearly four. On top of that Annette and I are leaders here and needed.

"My suggestions can be debated but I want representatives for the Camps and the Caves along. Therefore I'd like Brin and Benton. Yes, Brin, Cindy would come with you. Benton, your children are old enough to stay here if you want to bring Breanna."

"I would like that," Benton said. "So would she. I know that you will have adequate supervision for them and they are very nearly adults."

"I would like to go but only if grandfather approves," Brin said. "If he feels Thi would be better I will step aside."

"I approve," Neram said. "Thi still has little fear of anything though I think marriage to Ally will change that. You have learned the value of fear and the meaning of courage."

Brin nodded. "Thank you, grandfather. I will do my best."

"Who else are you thinking of," Grandpa asked.

"I would like a representative of the first family awake. It will be a difficult trip so I suggest Trevor and Amaya for that part of it."

"We accept," Trevor said after looking at his bride.

"I would like Abe and Jax to lead the mission. I suggest Nelson and Reilly for military/scout and I'd like Fred and Zane as chefs."

"Who is going as medic?" Grandma asked.

"I'd like to borrow Ian because he knows how to compound medications if they run out but I suggest Dr. Duff."

"I may not be the best choice," Dr. Duff demurred.

"You've learned a lot and you've changed a lot. I know you can do surgery as needed. You've also learned to hunt, forage, clean your kill and work the hide. Just about everyone is going to be doing at least one of those jobs."

"I can also get wood," Dr. Duff said. "Though it's a little hard on me to haul it."

"That I think you can skip," Brandon said. "We need you to be a doctor rather than need one."

"I think that's a good team and you're keeping it to a sensible size," Grandpa said.

"What are you going to take?"

"I would use the same setup as we did for the Climate People," Brandon said. "The exceptions would be all hover carts and we'd bring trade items. We can find out from Kalel what would be appropriate."

"You aren't planning on trading firearms are you?" Mr. Richards asked.

"No, definitely not during a first encounter," Brandon said. "We'll keep it simpler. Salt is always good, seeds, and other things that might be useful but not deadly."

"The biggest problem I see for your endeavor is winter preparations," Grandma said. "That's probably the easiest one to fix. We'll send a team of people to help out."

"That would be a great relief," Brandon said.

"What do you think we might find in that building?" Trevor asked.

"Considering all the things we could use I have no idea what to expect," Brandon said. "I do expect it to be useful."

Trade Items and Training

"How long will I be so limited?" Kalel asked from his wheelchair.

"It's been about three weeks since the avalanche. You aren't in as much pain so a minimum of three more weeks. We'll take the pins out and check progress. You may require either a cast or a splint after that for them to continue healing but you should be able to do limited walking then," Brandon replied.

"What am I going to do while I wait? Now that the medications are not keeping me asleep I have nothing to occupy my time."

"I don't suppose your people kept the memory of how to read?"

"What is reading?"

"That's what I thought. Reading is a way to communicate silently. As the Caves and Camps say they are small marks that tell us things. If you like you could join Ally, Thi and Brin. They're learning though they haven't progressed as far as some of our children."

"I would like that. It would be useful to know how to communicate without sound and as you are to be our teachers I am ready to learn anything you suggest."

"All right. Before I take you up there the council would like me to ask you a question. What would your people find useful in trades?"

"We have never traded outside our community but you do have a few things that would be highly prized. Your pink salt is one. We do have salt or can trade for it but the pink salt is unique. Your medicines are much more advanced, including the little pills you are giving me now. I know the taste but it is much better when it's not in a tea.

"You could also trade some of your unusual foods. I especially like the stringy stuff and the desserts."

"You mean pasta?"

"Yes, I believe that is what it's called."

"I'll have to teach one of the cooks going along how to make it and the desserts. I imagine one of the ones you like is chocolate."

"Is that the brown stuff?"

"Yes."

"Definitely."

After this conversation Brandon went to find Trevor.

"I have an addition to your duties on the mission," he told the young man. "Kalel says that some of our 'unusual food' would make good trade items. He's particularly meaning pasta and chocolate. As you already know a bit of how to work with chocolate I'm going to teach you a bit more and I'm going to teach you to make pasta."

"It's a good thing mom and Grandma made sure I know the basics of cooking, then," Trevor replied. "When do we start?"

"I've set up the second kitchen for classes. Noah and Tony will help in the beginning before they go back. Do you already know how to make sauce?"

"I can make basic tomato sauce and I know how to make 'mother' sauces. I'd need instruction on how to dress them up."

"That's good. Tony had to start with teaching me how to chop an onion without chopping my fingers."

Trevor reported to the kitchen and Brandon headed off to find Dr. Duff.

"Grandma wants to see you," he told the man. "I think she's going to give you a crash course in how to compound medicines so you can help Ian."

"I look forward to it," Dr. Duff said.

"Before we start," Grandma said when the man came into the lab, "do you have any questions or comments about plant based medicine?"

"I used to. I thought it was all quackery. However I've learned a great deal since then."

"There was a time when some people took advantage of others claiming to have cure-alls. Usually they were little more than grain alcohol, sometimes with pungent but ineffective herbs. Before the snake oil sales people and before true scientific study there were a lot of beliefs that proved to be dangerously inaccurate.

"However, when herbs were brought into the laboratory we made great strides in many ways. A lot of orthodox medicine was still being made from plants."

"Yes, Brandon taught me that and of course I knew about the snake oil types. I just thought, at the time, that was everyone involved."

"Thankfully, no. Now, has Brandon shown you how to make medicine?"

"Not really. He's been so busy with the Later People thing that he hasn't had time."

"The first things I'm going to show you are very simple to do. As you can see we have a scale. We use this to determine precisely how much of an herb or combination of herbs goes into each capsule. Brandon doesn't have the set up to make pills, though he has traded for most of the standard ones."

Dr. Duff and Grandma spent several days working on compounding various medications and treatments. He was surprised at her knowledge and glad to know more about taking care of people post the pharmaceutical era.

Trevor also spent a great deal of time learning. By the time spring arrived he was an adept cook, including making all of the items on his list over a camp fire and solar oven.

The guests returned to their homes after a two week visit and everyone was delighted with the results.

"Which way should we go?" Abe asked Kalel. "Is it along the route where you camped?"

"Yes, it is a two day walk from there."

"It won't take us that long to get there. We will probably get there in a few hours. Do you keep sentries?"

"Yes, we do. Not so much against people, though we do have a few that wake up and wander around in our territory. They have a hard time adapting to our ways."

"I would imagine. I'm guessing they find themselves in trouble because they want to use technology?"

"Some do. Most are grateful to have a community to belong to."

"So we can expect to be shot at when we arrive?"

"It depends on whether or not they believe you are the Later People. Our group would have told them what they saw."

"I think we'll have everyone in the hover carts when we approach. Amaya got knocked off her board, though it might have been surprise that did it."

"When are we leaving?"

"Tomorrow morning. I'm going to check on the equipment we're bringing next."

"I would like to see it and understand how it works. I may be able to help my people better that way."

"Sure, let's go to the cart garage."

When the two arrived at the garage Gavin was fussing with the placement of equipment.

"I came to check on the loading process," Abe said. "Kalel would like to know what each one does."

"I'm putting cargo in each cart but the heaviest stuff will go in our new wagon. That would be the solar refrigerator, freezer and oven."

"What do they do?" Kalel asked.

"We can keep some food cold, some of it will be frozen and we can use the oven to bake things," Abe explained. "Some of our medicines need to be kept cold as well, so they will be in the refrigerator."

"What are you bringing that is frozen?"

"Seafood, butter, chicken and milk. That way we have them for most of the trip. If any of your people are close enough to one of our communities we can probably resupply but I rather doubt they do."

"No, we would have met you before now. We had heard rumors via the Caves that you were up north. There is some trading now and then with them. It is not smiled upon but I think it's a good thing."

"Which cart are the trade items in?" Abe asked Gavin.

"There are some in each. The salt being the heaviest puts it in the wagon. The chocolate is in the refrigerator just in case it gets hot."

"Good, though it's somewhat doubtful. Tents and sleeping bags are in there as well?"

"Yes and the camp kitchen stuff. Zane and Fred came by earlier and loaded what they needed. So did Trevor."

"Good. I guess we're about ready then. I'm glad you're coming with us. If we run into trouble we're going to need someone who knows how to fix these things."

The next morning the team was fare welled on their mission. Trevor was excited and Dr. Duff was worried.

"You'll do just fine," Ian told him. "You're an excellent doctor and between us we should be able to handle almost anything."

"I never thought I would be on any sort of mission when I went into medicine. I hope I can keep up to expectations."

"You will."

Jax turned to Kalel who was beside her in the lead cart.

"Which way?" she asked.

"We walked along the river until we came to the creek."

"So basically southwest. How far along the river?"

"It's about a day's walk."

"We'll be there in less than two hours, then. Can we expect hunters to be out?"

"Yes, though most of the animals are very thin still. We don't feed them the way you do."

"So shields up from the beginning, then."

Within the two hours they came in site of a small village. Almost immediately arrows were bouncing off the force fields.

"It is the Later People," one man cried out.

"I hope that means they'll stop shooting," Trevor said. "It's kind of distracting when I'm trying to drive."

"They seem to have," Abe said. "There's a group of them in the clearing in the middle. Let's park there."

"Do we get out?" Amaya asked.

"Let me get out first," Kalel said.

"It's Kalel!" a woman exclaimed.

"Yes, I am home. I was severely injured and the Later People saved my life, my arm and my leg."

Kalel rolled up his sleeve to show the scars from the surgery to repair his broken arm.

"Are they here to meet us?" a man asked.

"Yes, Layel, they are. They can also trade and they have skilled medical people and medicine with them."

Kalel turned and motioned for the team to get out. They went to the group and introductions were made.

"Some of us thought that the Later People were a myth," Layel said. "It is somewhat difficult to see a myth come to reality before our eyes."

"I imagine it would be," Abe said. "We are called the Wakers because we wake up those sleeping in the cryo cases."

"That fulfills more of the myth. When you get to our strange building most will believe... as long as you can open the doors."

"I suspect we'll be able to," Abe said. "Especially if there's a notebook."

"You know of the Notebook?"

"You could say that. Each group, with the exception of Congress, has one. It tells us what we need to know about the sleepers and about any buildings that we find or need to make."

"Can you make sense of the tiny marks in it?"

"Yes, all of us can. If it's not too technical Kalel can now do so."

Layel turned to Kalel.

"They have taught you?"

"Yes, and they have taught me a great deal more about numbers."

"We should prepare a feast to celebrate this wondrous day," Layel said. "Will you join us?"

"We would be happy to. We can provide some of the food and if you need our doctors to visit anyone, we can do that as well," Abe said. "Where would you like us to set up our camp?"

"Here is fine. When other villages come to trade this is where they stay."

Abe turned to his team. "Trevor, you and Amaya gather wood. Take a cart so we don't deplete what's close by. Kalel, would you like to go with them? That way if they run into any hunters they might not be shot."

"We do not have any hunters out today," Layel said. "We have enough from winter so we're letting the animals gain weight."

"That is wise. We brought food for now so we do have things to share. However they're going to need a fire to cook it."

"I will go with them. I know where there is a good deal of dead fall. It's too far for us to go by foot but with these carts we'll be fine," Kalel said.

"Cindy, Brin, Thi and Ally please set up camp. Zane, you and Fred set up the camp kitchen. Trevor may want the oven, at least I'm hoping he does. Dr. Duff, you and Ian can see any patients that may be needing help."

"Mina is our medicine woman. She will be glad to show you who might need assistance."

At first Mina was a bit jealous of the two doctors but by the time the feast was ready she was singing their praises.

"I had never thought of sewing a wound closed," she told Dr. Duff. "What is in the oil that you used?"

The two continued in discussion for the entire feast.

"I haven't seen Mina this happy in a long time," Layel told Abe. "She carries the burden of our illnesses and injuries. She has high status but it is at a cost. It's like she hurts when one of us does."

"Grandma would say that it is the sign of a good healer," Abe replied. "She is one of the first Wakers to get out of the cryo cases and is our most senior medical person as well as a senior leader. Her grandson is the one who made dessert."

"Is she your grandmother?"

"No, but she and her husband have been called Grandma and Grandpa since they woke up. I don't even know what their other names were."

"Some of your food is strange. What is this that we are eating?" Layel asked as he was served the dessert.

"I made a couple of chocolate cakes," Trevor said. "Kalel seemed to think you would like it."

"I do like it but I've never tasted any cake like this. Our cakes are usually not light even if they are sweet."

"We have a number of things that will allow them to rise," Trevor explained. "I used eggs, baking soda, baking powder and salt with white flour."

"Now that we're done eating would you like to see some of the equipment we use?" Abe asked.

"Absolutely.

After looking over the solar cooking equipment they moved on to the hover carts and boards.

"Do these also use the sun for power?" Layel asked as an excited crowd gathered round.

"Yes but they have batteries that store power for use when it's cloudy or at night. The moon can help recharge when it's full but it's not as strong," Abe explained.

"What makes your arrows fall away from your crafts?" a young man asked.

"Jai..." Layel began.

"Ah, I have heard your name before, young man," Abe said.

Jai blushed but waited for an answer to the question.

"These crafts use a type of magnetic field that repels most objects. The field protects the craft and the people/things in them."

"Where have you heard Jai's name before?" Layel asked.

"Once when I followed him and his fellow spy after he shot Cindy and the second time was in council after he fired an arrow at Amaya. Fortunately she was learning to ride a board at the time and had the force field up."

Jai turned even redder. "Yeah and I got into a lot of trouble both times," he muttered.

"As you should have but the matter is over and done with," Abe said. "We do not hold grudges."

"We would," Layel said.

"It is not our way."

"The Wakers have many strange beliefs. My wife and I have joined them and approve of their beliefs. If we did not Kalel would have died," Benton said.

"You are from the Caves," Layel said.

"I was from the Caves. I am a Waker now."

"Perhaps now would be a good time for a weapons demonstration," Jax said. "It may help them to understand why we don't feel a need to kill an enemy."

"You have weapons other than a bow?" Layel asked.

"We have several other weapons," Abe replied. "We use a slingshot, a tranquilizer gun, rifles and sometimes hand guns."

"I would like to see," Layel said.

"The only ones we don't use in demonstrations are the tranq guns," Jax said. "They put animals or people to sleep for several hours. That way we don't have to kill them."

"Do you use these weapons?" Jai asked Jax.

"I do. I have been hunting a long time. We prefer to use renewable arms such as the bow and the slingshot but larger animals need a higher powered weapon."

"This I must see," Jai said. "I know some women can hunt but it is very rare."

"I'm well aware of your opinion of women, young man," Jax told him. "I'm hoping it has undergone a change."

"It has. I do not like extra duty."

"Good. There is a pinecone in that tree," she said as she pointed. "I'll hit it with a bow."

The pinecone landed thirty feet away.

"Do you see that rock?" she pointed to one a hundred feet away. "Put the pinecone on it."

Jai did so, and when he returned Jax shattered it with a rifle.

"Can all of your women do that?" Jai asked in awe.

"All of our girls and women must be proficient with at least one weapon. Many are proficient in all four weapons. Trevor's fourteen year old cousin Jackie helped save a group of young children from coyotes last year with a tranq gun. She started learning the bow and slingshot when she was six."

"Is it true that your women and men have equal status?"

"We are equals. Even those of us in leadership positions help wash dishes... as do the men."

"You have much to teach us and not just Technology," Layel said.

"We have much to learn about you," Abe replied. "I would like to know more about your customs and culture."

"Before we talk, let me send runners to the rest of the villages. I have already told them what our people had seen but some were skeptical. It would be wise for them to know you are coming."

"We would appreciate that," Abe said.

Once the runners had been sent the two leaders sat down.

"As Kalel probably told you at the beginnings of our people a man told us that we were to wait for the Later People to teach us how to use Technology. He said that we were not ready for it and he left us a Notebook so that you could open the building we had been trying to get into.

"Over time several things became more rigid. At first it was just the Technology in the building but now it is any new Technology. There have been people put to death for devising a new way to do something. Others coming into our territory with new things were and are also attacked.

"It was also noted that women were not as strong physically as men. This has caused many to consider them of less status, though there have been and are exceptions. Mina is one. She has more status than some of the men, but it is expected because of her abilities.

"Your Technology will change that. Just watching your co-leader use weapons shows me that. This isn't going to please some of the men. However those men are not high status themselves mostly because of that attitude."

"How would you recommend we approach other villages?"

"As you did here though I cannot guaranty your safety. I fear there may be a split in our people. We've had all winter to get used to the idea and to hear the stories. The others have not."

"We'll do our best. Where would you recommend we go next?"

"The sooner you can get the doors to our building open the better. However there is another village between us and that one. Our runner to them earlier was harassed by a group of people though he was not injured."

"Should we stop there or go around?"

"I would counsel you to go around. Once the leaders at our central village accept you it will be hard for the rest of them to do less than otherwise."

"That said we'll keep the force fields up as I imagine there will be sentries along the way."

"That is true and possibly hunters. It was quite amazing to watch the arrows fall away before striking anything. I'm sure it will cause quite a stir."

"You said something about a split in your people. Is there any way to avoid it?"

"I doubt it. It's almost inevitable. Change and acceptance is hard enough for me and I am a relatively young man. The older people will not want change and those who have little status would likely follow them."

"I'm glad we have the tranquilizer guns."

"Putting them to sleep for a few hours will not change their minds."

"No, but it would make it possible to ensure they don't have any weapons to hurt others with. We've found that most people are open-minded once they get over their fears."

"I hope so. If not your medical team will be very busy."

"I hope there's an operating room in that building..."

The Strange Building

"That was one scary ride," Amaya said. "I'm glad they don't have guns."

"Yeah, we'll have to be careful about that. I'd prefer that they don't get any for a while," Abe replied. "I see the building and it is a bunker. There are also a lot of cases around it. I wonder what we should do first, open the building or the cases."

"I'd open the building," Kalel said. "The faster that's done the safer we all are."

"Ok. Let's park these carts and meet the villagers."

"I'd rather not get out until they stop firing arrows at us," Trevor said.

"As they aren't hitting us they'll have to. Either that or go get more ammo," Gavin replied. "Yep, they've stopped."

Kalel got out and spoke to the leaders.

"These are the Later People. They are here to see the Notebook and to open the building," he said.

"If they can do that I will accept they are the Later People," the leader said.

"Thank you, Nali. I know they can do this." He motioned the team to get out.

"Here is the Notebook," Nali said after a young man had gone to get it.

"Wow, it's old," Trevor said as he looked over Abe's shoulder. "There's the door code."

"Ok, let's get this part of things over with," Jax said. "Who gets to punch in the code?"

"Probably it would be best of if Abe did it," Trevor said. "He is a leader and they may have problems at first with female co-leaders."

"I don't know," Abe said. "I think you should do it, Jax. Let them know we Later People don't think women are second class."

"Ok. Let me see the code."

After Jax entered the code the doors slowly creeped open. Emergency lights came on and the crowd behind the team gasped.

"I hope we wake up a couple of pilots," Trevor said. "I don't think any of us know how."

"We probably will and there are always the notebooks," Abe said. "Let's see what else is inside."

"I think we get our wish in the medical department," Amaya said. "Medications, equipment and that door is labeled "OR."

"Good, we need one that's closer than Chesapeake or Congress," Ian said.

"There are more hover craft and repair equipment plus spare parts," Gavin reported from further ahead.

"They have freezers," Zane said. "Stocked with that freeze dried food."

"They have a full kitchen," Fred said.

"They also have room for two or three hundred people," Cindy reported.

"We may end up setting up another community," Trevor said with a grin.

"As long as we're not caught in a full-fledged war," Abe reminded him. "That would make things difficult for all involved."

The leaders of the village had followed the team as they looked over what was in the building.

"You know how to use these things?" Nali asked.

"We know how to use almost everything and we know what the copters are. The sleepers around the building probably know how to fly them."

"They fly? Like birds?"

"Yes, some can go much higher than birds. They also go very fast."

"That is a wonder. I believe you are the Later People. We look forward to learning from you."

�

The Split

When they got outside they could see two groups of people. Most of them were talking excitedly about what had just happened but another group was staring malevolently at the 'outsiders.'

"Uh-oh, I think we have problems," Trevor murmured.

"Layel was afraid of something like this," Jax murmured back.

Nali raised his hand and both groups quieted.

"They have used the Notebook and opened the doors. They are the Later People. We welcome them."

"They can't be the Later People," a member of the hostile group said. "I see one from the Caves and others from the Camps. They are not Later People."

"Omri, they have my countenance. They have proved themselves. The Later People will teach us many things and that may well include getting along with and/or joining other groups. You have already seen that they treat their women as equals."

"I don't agree with that, either. Women are not equals. They aren't strong enough and could not survive without men."

"Your treatment of the women in your life has gotten you into trouble many times, Omri. You do not want to continue down that path."

"Leave me out of that. What is important is that I am obviously not the only one who thinks this way."

"I am leader of the most respected village we have. What you think is not in line with what I have decreed. It is not in line with what the majority of the village believes. You do not get to decide this matter."

"We'll see about that. There are going to be many people like us. You had better prepare for that."

"You will have extra duty today, Omri. If there is any violence towards the Later People or those of us who believe you will have more than that."

Nali turned to Abe. "Those who are disagreeing are all either low status people like Omri or those who most fervently resist change. Because of that they are also lower status. Nothing remains the same forever."

"I'm glad you feel that way," Abe replied. "Layel felt there would be problems with other villages. His seems to be a hundred percent in favor."

"What should we do next?"

"We're going to set up camp and make some stew. Then we will wake up some of the sleepers. I doubt we could do all of them in one day. There are at least a hundred of them. Thankfully they can use the barracks in the bunker for a place to stay."

"You may want to wait a day or two before you wake them up. Omri has a violent temper and I don't know what he might decide to do."

"Good point. We do keep sentries and we have a weapon that will put an attacker to sleep for several hours."

"That is better than killing them though I am afraid someone is going to get hurt. Layel is an astute man and has potential to be a major leader."

"Speaking of people who are hurt we have doctors with us. Do you have any members who need help?"

"We always have a few. Our medicine man is on the side of the unbelievers so he may not be willing to work with your doctors."

"We'll deal with that when we come to it. Ian, Dr. Duff, Nali will take you to see those who are ill or injured. At least now we have proper facilities if something major is needed."

In order to prevent people from going into the building without Waker permission Abe and the others set up camp directly in front of it.

"Park the hover carts and wagon in there as well," Jax said. "That should prevent them from being tampered with."

"Are we sharing a meal with them today?" Frank asked.

"I don't know. Things could devolve into a fight pretty fast," Jax said.

"If we are invited we will share. If not we will invite the leader and any who he thinks would be helpful in cooling this situation down to our meal," Abe replied.

"It's a good thing we don't need to go hunting or foraging," Cindy said. "Omri is still talking to that group and they're glaring our direction a lot."

"They're glaring at everybody a lot," Benton said. "I can tell where Nali is just by watching which way their heads swivel."

"We'll have to have sentries and perhaps have them during the day," Nelson said. "I don't think Mr. Hothead over there is necessarily going to wait for nightfall if he can find a way before then."

"Too bad we don't have force fields to go around the camp," Amaya said with a shiver.

Nali and the two doctors returned.

"Even if you hadn't been able to open the doors I would believe after what I just saw," Nali said. "All of those your doctors saw are doing much better."

"They weren't too badly off," Dr. Duff said. "Some of the things we have we've found in the various crates. There are also probably quite a few medications in the bunker. We'll have to inventory them later."

"Would you care to share a meal with us?" Nali asked.

"We would like that though we will probably leave guards here," Abe said. "If someone who doesn't know what they are doing tries to use some of our equipment they might get hurt."

"That is a wise precaution. I will also provide you with guards."

"We will bring some of our food so you can try it. These are things you can learn to make and they will improve your health and make other foods go further," Jax said.

"That sounds wonderful. I will tell our people to prepare food for a feast."

Those of the villagers that had sided with Omri did not participate in the feast. Omri was only present doing his extra duty, which appeared to be hauling firewood so the cooks could work. Benton and Reilly stayed to guard their camp.

When they returned from the feast Reilly reported that several people had approached the camp but seeing it guarded by four people had aborted their attempts to get closer.

"It's going to be a long night," Nelson said. "You two get something to eat. We brought back food for you and the village guards also have food saved for them. Brin and I will guard now."

"Are we going to have help guarding all night?" Cindy asked.

"I don't know," Abe said. "It wouldn't surprise me. Nali doesn't want any incidents any more than we do."

At that point Nali came to the camp with eight men.

"I know you will have guards but we would like to help. These men will come in pairs and watch with your watchers. I don't think they will try anything tonight but Omri has sent some of those on his side to do something. It may be to gather support for his view of things."

"What will you do if he manages to do that?" Abe asked.

"It will depend on what they do. If they start violence it will go badly for everyone."

"I'll send word to the other Wakers. If it does start violence we will help you resolve it as fast as possible."

"We would appreciate that. I think you will need more warriors."

"Not to mention more doctors, food and medical supplies," Jax said.

"The joint councils will know what and who to send," Benton said.

The night was a restless one for almost everyone. Abe had informed Home Base about the situation and was told that he would receive word in the morning. Shortly after breakfast Grandpa called on the radio.

"We're going to send you several key people," Grandpa said. "Sarge, Henry, Henderson, Dr. Hadon and thirty volunteers with various skills. You'll be getting several medics and of course everyone knows how to handle weaponry.

"You are advised to find or build a defensible space. A bunker isn't exactly built that way. Check the crates to see if there are any house kits. If there are let us know and we'll send Nathan and Johnson. Only unmarried people are going male or female. I had a fight on my hands with that one but there are enough to get the job done.

"I imagine you're going to need more food. Grandma, Heather and Alderson are making up care packages. The Gap wanted to but as they need to concentrate on winter preps I told them no. We're also sending more ammo, including tranquilizer darts."

"We can do that. This is likely to be a shooting type event. I'm not so much worried about us as I am about the villagers. They will shoot and be shot at."

"That's understood. When you mentioned the emphasis on status both Ruth and Neram became very concerned. Apparently those with low status may feel they have nothing to lose and everything to gain. They will shoot and they will shoot at you."

"Agreed. We'll get onto the defensible space immediately. We may have a little time."

"Keep us updated, Home Base out."

After this conversation Abe turned to the team.

"Trevor, Brin and Thi start checking crates and look for housebuilding materials. There probably are some and they're probably close to the bunker. If you find any come and tell me immediately.

"Jax, you and Gavin go as guards for them. Nelson, you and Reilly please guard the camp. Cindy, you and Amaya back them up. I'm going to talk to Nali."

Everyone went their separate directions. The two doctors went into the bunker to start looking over the medical supplies and equipment. Kalel went with them.

"I'm glad to see you," Nali said when Abe approached. "I was on my way to your camp."

"What happened?"

"In the night all of those on Omri's side left. They took food, weapons and shelter... not all of which were theirs for the taking. I've sent trackers out to look for them and find out what's going on. I'm guessing they sent runners to other villages looking for like-minded people and found some."

"That would be my guess. The joint councils are sending food, medicine and reinforcements. They're also bringing us more ammunition. We will be building a house if we can find a kit for it. This will give us more defensible space against an attack. In a way it's probably a good thing that they aren't here to see us build."

At this point one of the trackers came back.

"What have you found?" Nali asked.

"We have found the place they have met up," Payel said. "There are about three hundred of them, men and women."

"Are they armed?"

"All of the men and a few of the women are armed. They are all low status people. Quami is the only medicine man they have."

"As Quami is also not especially good at being a medicine man they will have problems," Nali said in a dry tone.

"Did you overhear their plans?"

"Rani is staying to listen. Right now they are still setting up camp. Omni has three others gathered round him but so far the orders are for setting up sentries, gathering wood and so forth. One thing is clear, they are very eager to rise. I think Omni thinks he will become chief leader. I am to go back as soon as I can."

"Take Tasel with you. We will need two spies round the clock. With three of you there one can stay while the other reports back if one of you is hurt or captured."

"Yes, Nali." Payel took off at a jog trot to find Tasel and to gather supplies for a long wait.

"Omni is an ambitious man but does not have the discipline to rise in rank. He's only adequate with a bow, he's an indifferent hunter and he has no other skills," Nali told Abe.

Trevor came up and waited for an opening.

"Did you find a kit?" Abe asked.

"Three of them though I suspect you'd rather us concentrate on one right now."

"Yes, tell the others to get started. I'll pull the doctors out of the bunker to help and radio for them to send Nathan and Johnson."

"Yes, sir."

By the time Sarge arrived the house was framed. Nathan and Johnson were on their way. Everyone was wary and had the force fields up on their crafts.

"Good work," Sarge said. "I'd like to meet with Nali and tell you some of the other suggestions from the joint council," he told Abe.

"He's nearby," Abe said. "In fact, here he comes. He must have heard a strange voice."

"Good observer," Sarge replied.

"Nali, this is Sarge. He has more recommendations from the joint council."

"First thing is they want all noncombatants in the bunker for the duration. If you have people who are too young, too old or don't know how to use a bow they need to be moved to safety. Ruth was adamant on that. Apparently you guys don't mind taking out women and children if you consider them enemies."

"For many of us that would be true. I agree and will start that process immediately. What will they need?"

"Food, clothing and any medications they take. Stuff to keep them occupied. We can resupply as needed and a few of us will be in there in other capacities if they need help."

Nathan and Johnson pulled up at that point. Sarge nodded as they went straight for the house to begin their part of the work.

"What are those men going to do?" Nali asked.

"Johnson is going to do the plumbing for the house. That means it will have running water and a way for waste water to be disposed of. Nathan will wire it for electricity and set up the solar panels. That will provide light, heat, a means to cook and other amenities."

"That would be good, to have all of those things without being dependent on going to a well or using candles."

"It's a lot safer and better for the environment as well. I'd like to meet with the people who are going to be your main defenders. I'd also like to show you how our weapons work. I don't want anyone to be surprised when we fire our rifles. Henderson didn't get much sleep last night and has agreed to be the target for the tranquilizer gun."

"What will that do to him?"

"He'll sleep for about six hours. Smaller people might sleep longer but it's still safe."

The demonstrations were set up and performed. After Henderson was asleep Trevor and Reilly carried him into the bunker to sleep off the effects.

"That is a brave man," Nali said. "I would also like to learn more about both of those weapons at some point. Putting an enemy to sleep may have more value than killing him."

"That's what we think. Many times the enemy is someone who does not understand us or our ways. Once they've had a time to cool off and appreciate the benefits they often become friends and allies."

Sarge called Abe and Jax to join the conversation.

"They have about a hundred people who are good with a bow. Another fifty are what Nali calls adequate. I'm going to watch them do some practice shots. We've added over forty more and have the advantage of the tranq guns. There may be more of them but not all of them can shoot."

"It sounds like we have the advantage," Abe said. "Are there any more reports from the spies?"

"Our watchers say they did not even post sentries last night. Omri had a temper fit over that so they are likely to have watchers tonight.

"He is having his bowmen practice. He isn't practicing, he's watching. The watchers say that the men may not be deadly but they will definitely be able to injure people. A lucky strike could kill. I hope you have something to treat the smelly, deadly aftereffects of such a wound?"

"Yes, we can do many things to prevent infections," Jax replied. "We have everything we need with us and more is available in the bunker."

"Abe do you want to assess our 'adequate' warriors with me?" Sarge asked.

"Yes, I would. I think the house will be up and functioning late today and I've already set folks to work on the trees."

"What are you going to do with trees?" Nali asked.

"We post half of our sentries in them. They aren't visible but they can see further away and can still fire if needs be," Abe explained.

"Clever. We would never look up and the tree limbs would make them nearly impossible to see."

"That's why we're glad they left before we got started," Jax said. "They won't know."

By the end of the day the building was completed enough to be used.

"Let's not break camp," Abe suggested. "We don't have to be in the tents but they might think we are."

"What good would that do?" Amaya asked. "Not that I mind not having another chore."

"They would be less likely to consider the house or the trees a major point of interest," Sarge replied. "Not a bad idea. The sentries can add wood to the fire as well."

⋯

Enemy on the Move

Three days later Rani, one of the watchers, reported that the other warriors were on the move.

"Are the other two tracking them?" Nali asked.

"It isn't that hard of a job," Rani said. "They have little hunting skills and they move through the forest like a herd of cattle."

"How should we handle this," Nali asked Abe.

"What are they likely to do?"

"Wait until they think we're all asleep and then attack. They might set fire to some of the cabins or your camp."

"Or both. Do you think they will watch us?"

"I'm sure of it."

"All right. We will act like this is a typical day. When it grows dark I'd like your best warriors on the rooves of the cabins and other buildings. The rest of us will pretend to be asleep but we'll be armed and awake."

"Will you be in your camp?"

"No, it's too vulnerable. We have blanket rolls that make it look like we are. Our fighters will be on top of the bunker, in the trees and on the rooves with your men."

"Won't anyone fight on the ground?"

"If we have to, but it would be far too easy for us to be hit by one of our own bullets, arrows or darts."

"What of our other warriors?"

"They have the hardest and most dangerous task. Some of my men will be with them for it. They will be in the darkness between the cabins and beside the bunker in order to prevent as much destruction as possible."

"They will gain much status."

"They will save lives and property which is more important than status, but if they do it will be a good thing."

"Why don't you want our best warriors for that task?"

"Your best warriors can hit what they aim for so there's less risk of them hitting one of us or your other men."

"That's true. The ones on the ground can only hit those on the ground."

"Exactly."

When Abe reported the strategy to Sarge he approved. "On the ground I suggest Henderson, Reilly, Johnson and me. I'd like you to be in charge of the tree sentries. Nelson can be in charge on the top of the bunker. Trevor can be in charge on the ground level."

"I'd like our women to be in the trees. They're great shots and it will be safer. Amaya will kick up a fuss and Cindy might also. If they do they can go on the bunker which is a little more dangerous."

"None of us are going to be safe. I'd rather they were in the bunker instead of on it but we need the fighters."

Sure enough several women objected to being in the safest spot for the coming battle.

"You do realize you would also be in a key position, right?" Trevor asked Amaya.

"True. Why can't I be on the bunker? That's pretty safe as well."

"That's up to Nelson," Sarge said.

"I'll take Cindy and Amaya because I know their skill levels. I'd also like Brin and Kalel. You can assign more if you think more are needed."

"I will because I do," Sarge said. "Who do you want, Trevor?"

"Definitely Thi and Gavin. Nathan is also pretty good. As with Nelson you can assign others to me as I don't know some of them."

"All medical personnel should be in the bunker until the fighting is over. This is going to probably be a brief battle. The aftermath will take a lot longer."

The Battle

"They're coming," Rani whispered to Nali and Abe. He slipped into the shadows between two cabins to take his position as a defender.

Abe was concerned about all of the people he was leading into this fight. He'd hoped to avoid it but that was simply not possible. Now the best he could hope for was as few deaths as possible.

Brin was equally concerned. He'd never participated in a battle before. Shooting enemies with a tranquilizer gun from a position of safety and superiority was not the same as being out in the open, even if he was on top of a building. He wasn't shielded by trees this time. Would he have the courage to fight?

The attack came on two fronts. Abe heard a yell and saw their camp going up in flames. He also saw those lighting it collapsing from tranquilizer darts. Then he was too busy to pay attention to other areas. A barrage of arrows was coming at them. Arrows and tranq darts were flying from the rooves and between the cabins.

"Man down," Abe heard a voice say. It sounded like Sarge. "Man down," came over the radio five more times. He could see bodies everywhere, some falling off the rooves. As he concentrated he could see that those cabins were on fire.

Then it was over. The last of the enemy was down. Time to assess the damage.

"Who all has been hit?" Abe asked into the radio.

"Henderson," Sarge said. It sounded like he had a lump in his throat. "He's dead."

"Brin's injured. It looks serious," Nelson said.

"I've been hit and so has Thi," Trevor said through gritted teeth.

"Two people up here were hit but they're flesh wounds," Cindy said. "Do we need to stay at our posts?"

"You may accompany Brin," Abe said. "I'd like four people to stay in the trees, four on the ground and four on the bunker. The rest of you come and help sort the victims. Leave the sleepers until the injured have all been carried into the bunker. If they start to wake up we can tranq them again."

"We also need to put out the fires," Sarge said. "Nali has some people on it already. I'll organize some help. There were fire hoses in the bunker and there's a tap for it on the outside."

"Thanks, Sarge."

"Don't kill the injured," Abe bellowed just as someone was about to do that. "We'll heal them and we'll find a way to reform them if we can. There are too few people for us to kill each other off."

The sizzling sound was welcome as it meant the fires were going out but moans and screams continued. Abe felt pain in his left thigh but ignored it as he helped bring the injured into the bunker for treatment.

When the last man had been brought in Dr. Hadan looked at Abe.

"Did you know you have an arrow in your thigh? There's blood all down your leg."

"Is everybody accounted for?"

"Yes."

"Good. I'll wait until it's my turn but I think I'm going to have to sit down."

"No," Ian said. "You're going to have to lie down. Triage wise your wound is next."

"I have to contact Grandma and Grandpa…" Ian gave him an injection and the next thing he knew Grandma was leaning over him.

"Back with us? You gave us a bit of a scare," she said.

"I did? How long was I out? What's going on? When did you get here?"

"Two days, mostly because you wouldn't lie still. The arrow hit the femoral artery and you lost quite a lot of blood before you came in. If you hadn't come in then it's possible you would have died. The fact that it stayed in your leg is probably what saved your life but even then it's a miracle."

"What's going on?"

"Brin is finally conscious. He was shot by an arrow and fell off the top of the bunker. I finally convinced Cindy to go to bed. The news that Brin had been seriously injured was bad for Neram. He's doing a little better now that he's talked to his grandson.

"Trevor's wounds required surgery but he's recuperating. Amaya had the sense to move a cot into his room once he was out of danger. Thi's wound needed stitches. Omri is in critical condition. The medicine man, Quami, is dead."

"Sarge told me about Henderson. How many others died?"

"Eighty-five. Seventy-five were the attackers, ten were from the LP. Before you ask, two others of our people were slightly wounded, one hundred twenty-five of the attackers were wounded and twenty-five of the LP. Fifty of the attackers were tranqued."

"What about the cabins?"

"Four cabins were partially burned. One of them is Nali's. He's staying in the bunker for the moment. Your camp was destroyed but it was clever of you to keep it up and let it be a target. It saved lives."

"Have all the patients been seen to?"

"Yes, and the doctors are rotating now so they can get some rest. I've helped a little but there are enough of them now that I'm not needed."

"Back to my third question… when did you get here?"

"Yesterday. We spent some of the time day before yesterday rounding up doctors and taking care of Neram."

"Good. When can I get up?"

"Not yet. Probably in time for the funerals which will be this evening. The LP people are similar to all of us in the eulogy. Trevor and Amaya will be doing Taps even though he'll be stuck in a wheelchair. You probably will be as well."

"What are we going to do with Omri?"

"I think it will depend largely on what he says once he's able to be interviewed. I have suggested that he go before the joint council. Nali is thinking about it."

"You know that the Caves and Camps will vote death."

"Yes. I'm just glad Benton and Breanna were unharmed. It would make things worse."

?

Burials

When Abe was wheeled out of the bunker he could see the neat rows of graves. Someone had sprinkled dirt over the blood though the smell lingered along with the smell of smoke. When everyone had assembled Nali spoke first.

"I would like to speak of many things. We honor bravery and many of those who lie here were brave. Many of you listening to my words were brave. All of the fighters have gained status.

"I say all because I believe that many of those fighting against us were misled. A few acted out of greed or malice. Most were inflamed by an idea that they might have welcomed had they not been encouraged to fight against it. There will be redemption for those who were misled.

"I think that this proves that we need the Later People. None of those dead or wounded were hit by them. They fired a weapon that caused them to fall asleep. That got them out of the battle without killing."

Nali sat down and Sarge stood up to speak.

"I have known most of our people from the time we woke up. One of the fighters actually helped wake us up. That is seven years ago now.

"I knew Henderson before we went into cryogenic sleep. He was one of my trusted men. I knew I could always rely on him to follow orders unless he had good cause not to. Since we woke up he proved himself over and over for all of us.

"I would also like to talk about bravery. The men and women who fought this battle were brave. In case you didn't know we had ten women who fought alongside everyone else. They didn't have to but there was no way to convince them not to do their part. It is one of the ways we Wakers have grown into such a strong community.

"Good night, Henderson. We'll see you on that bright morning."

Grandpa noticed tears on Sarge's cheeks when he got up to speak. Sarge was not ashamed of them.

"Henderson was one of Sarge's men who stayed at Home Base. Because we didn't have a lot of military at first we had to spread them out rather thin. That doesn't mean Henderson's only job was to guard us.

"He was adept with a hammer, a good hunter and a community leader. He could be gentle with those who had difficulty waking up and firm with those who didn't want to do their share of the work that needed done... without raising his voice.

"Until we were able to train horses to pull our carts he was one of the men we knew could handle pulling a loaded cart for miles. He very rarely complained and when he did it was usually about something that needed to be fixed.

"Henderson, you will be missed, my friend."

Abe was wheeled over to speak.

"We Wakers, we Later People, have stood by you in your time of need. We have been injured and one has died for you. As Nali said we did not kill anyone. We didn't need to kill anyone.

"Battles like this are not necessary. There are other ways to resolve issues. The pain I feel as the person who led my team into a battle in which they were killed and injured will stay with me forever. It is a pain that no one should have to feel again.

"As we bury these honored dead, let us remember that. Killing is a permanent solution to a temporary problem."

Abe nodded to Trevor and Amaya who sang the song played at so many funerals.

Day is done
Gone the sun
From the hills
From the lakes
From the skies
All is well
Safely rest
God is nigh.

Section Three Omri and the Wakeup

"Omri is conscious," Ian told Abe. "He wants to speak to you."

"Wouldn't it be better if it was Grandpa?" Abe asked.

"No, he was specific. You are the leader of the battle and the leader of the team."

"All right. He's good and pinned down?"

"He's not going anywhere for a while. We had to resuscitate him as it is."

Abe walked into the curtained cubicle. The man he saw on the bed was a far cry from the warrior who had defied his leader.

"I am sorry," he whispered. "I have seen a vision while I was asleep. It troubles me greatly. However I know now that you are the Later People and that what I did was wrong."

Abe sat down. "Did the vision tell you that?"

"No, the vision is another matter. It would take an Elder to explain it. I know because of how badly I was injured and because you did not kill me. Instead you are healing me. Not even the greatest medicine person of all of our people could have done it."

"Has anyone told you the results of the battle?"

"No. I think they fear it will harm me. It won't because I saw a good deal of it in my vision. I know one of your people was killed, that you and two more were seriously injured and that more than eight tens of our people were killed."

"Yes, plus quite a few wounded. Some are still in critical condition."

"If I had not fanned the flames this would not have happened."

"You'd have to talk to Grandpa on that one. I don't know that I agree."

"Would Grandpa be able to explain a vision?"

"Most likely. If he couldn't Grandma probably could."

"They are both Elders?"

"If I understand how you're using that word, yes. They are also older people. Grandma is fifty-seven and Grandpa is sixty."

"I would like to speak to Grandpa."

"I'll let him know."

Abe went in search of Grandpa and explained the strange interview he'd just had.

"I'm gathering you didn't mention that one of the seriously wounded was Trevor?" Grandpa asked.

"No, but he may know. I've heard of near death experiences."

"I probably am the best one to talk to him, then. I won't tell him but if he knows it will be interesting."

Grandpa noticed the pallor of Omri's face. Grandma had given him a graphic description of the man's injuries which included two arrows in his torso and another in his thigh.

"You asked to see me?" he asked the man in a gentle voice.

"Are you Grandpa?"

"Yes, that's what everyone calls me."

"But you are also a grandfather. One of the injured people has your look."

"Yes, that would be my grandson."

"Are you going to kill me?"

"No, I don't wish for you to be killed."

"Why?"

"Because I don't believe in killing people. I believe in healing people."

"Is that why you came?"

"Yes. Abe told me you'd had a vision and wanted to tell someone who could interpret it for you."

"Can you?"

"It's possible. I'd need to know the vision first."

"It was after I was brought inside. Suddenly I was floating near the ceiling. When I looked down I could see all kinds of people working on my body, yet I wasn't in it. Nearby were other people who had been injured and were being treated. That is how I saw your grandson.

"I went outside and I could see the rows of the dead. Graves were being dug and I wondered if one would be for me. Then I saw a light.

"I was drawn to that light like a moth to a candle. When I got near it a Man stopped me. I think he was The Man. He showed me a place of absolute beauty and a place of absolute torment. Then he said I must change or I would be in the place of torment."

"Your beliefs are very much like ours," Grandpa said. "The Caves and Camps are also similar. There is a major difference. We believe we must act as The Man acted for us."

"But He was killed!"

"And rose again. Your religion teaches that as well. I've talked with Nali."

"Yes, so that we might."

"Here is what He taught us. We are to love everyone and not hate anyone. That means that we are to love our family and also our enemies. We are to love those who hate us.

"We are to heal and avoid violence. We are to accept people, not reject them. We are to forgive and not seek revenge. If we don't do these things then we are not following Him. We are doing wrong."

"How can I know this is true?"

"I'm here, talking to you. Your wounds have been treated and our people kept your people from killing you. None of our people harmed your people even though yours harmed and killed us."

"That is a powerful thing to do."

"That power does not come from us. It comes from Him."

After reassuring the man Grandpa went in search of Abe.

"As far as we're concerned you are the ranking Waker leader here," Grandpa said. "Jax is your co-leader. A decision is going to have to be made about Omri because his actions have affected the Camps and other Waker communities."

Abe sighed. "I was afraid it would come to that. All right, I need a council, I need to know about this dream and I certainly hope you, Grandma and Sarge will be sitting in."

"Your team would be a good place to start and yes, we'll sit in. I think all of you should hear his vision. It will make a big difference, I suspect."

"I'll round them up. Until we find or wake up electricians and plumbers I'm going to want to borrow Johnson and Nathan. Most of us prefer sleeping above ground."

A few hours later the first meeting of the LP community began.

"As you know we're going to have to establish a community here," Abe began. "It's pretty obvious the cryo people considered this an important spot and we do have the responsibility of teaching the LP people.

"One of the first things we have to consider is Omri. Dr. Duff, how long before he can safely travel?"

"Next week would probably be the earliest. It's probably wise for you to wait longer before traveling. That was a serious injury."

"Ok, so if we don't reach a decision today we have time but I'd like to get it done. Before we address the issue Grandpa needs to tell us about a 'vision' he had while being treated. Most of you are familiar with the idea of near death experiences and I suspect we're going to hear about one."

"Yes, you are," Grandpa said. "He was able to see himself being worked on, those who were injured and the many that were killed, including Henderson. He recognized that Trevor was one of the injured because there is some resemblance between us.

"He was then drawn to a light and met a Man. The Man showed him heaven and hell. He was told that if he did not change he would be going to the latter.

"Their culture has the same basic tenets as ours, at least as regards religion. They believe in God and Jesus although He has a different name. I believe the Man was Jesus."

"If he believes in the Son why did he start this fight?" Benton asked.

"Because not everyone who says they believe follow what the Sacred Book says," Brin replied. "There was a time when I did not."

"Do you think he may be able to change?" Trevor asked. "This is one of the worst crimes we've had to deal with."

"That is a question you must decide. You may want to visit him before you make a decision. He will have to go before the joint councils because he caused serious harm to us and a member of our alliance," Grandpa said.

"I'd have to talk to him," Trevor replied. "But I'm willing to consider it."

"I think most of us would have to get a feel for whether or not he should be spared," Jax said.

"All right, but please do so one at a time and in the relatively near future," Abe said. "As for me I say give him a chance but I've already spoken with him."

"I agree with you," Brin said. "You have two votes for a chance now."

When the council met two days later a great deal had been accomplished. Aside from the council members meeting with Omri, two more houses had been completed, power and water in use and the LP people were astonished.

"Have you all had a chance to talk to Omri yet?" Abe asked.

"Yes," they all either said or nodded.

"Do you want to talk about it or just vote?"

"I would like to talk briefly," Benton said.

"You have the floor."

"I was surprised. The man we all saw before this battle is gone. This is a different man. He is humble. He knows he deserves to die. Normally I would say 'no chance,' but I cannot. I vote yes. Save him if you can."

Abe looked at the faces around him. Each person nodded.

"I think that sums it up fairly well," Abe said. "When he's given the all clear health wise we will go to the joint council and I will do my best for him."

"He will get a death verdict from Ruth," Benton warned.

"My grandfather may, also," Brin said.

"I think I know a way around that in this case," Abe said. "It's not one I'd have thought of before cryo but it very well might work."

"What are you going to do?" Grandma asked.

"As you'll be on the panel I think I'll reserve that for the trial. Let it be known that I will want to speak after the penalty phase."

"It is so noted," Grandpa said. "Whatever it is I hope it works."

Five days later Abe, Omri and those who had come from Home Base to help departed for the trial and to return home. Omri was quiet the entire ride but he did look around a great deal.

When they went before the councils Judge Benjamin pounded the gavel to call the trial to order.

"You are accused of inciting a rebellion that killed and wounded several Wakers and seriously injured a member of the Camps. How do you plead?"

"I am guilty, sir," Omri replied.

"Then we should debate the penalty. We will adjourn for two hours and tell you the penalty when we return."

Two hours and some heated debate later they returned.

"Waker communities have you come to an agreement?"

"Yes. Our sentence is twenty years hard labor but the sentence is suspended for the moment."

"Neram, have the Camps?"

"Yes. Death."

"Ruth?"

"We agree, death."

"A special request has been made that Abe speak to you before court is adjourned. Abe, the floor is yours."

"How many times must a man die?" Abe asked.

"A man can only die once," Ruth said.

"But, if a man stops breathing and his heart stops breathing he is dead, right?"

"I would agree with that," Ruth replied.

"That would define dead to me," Neram put in.

"And if that happens and we are able to bring him back does that mean your sentence has been met?"

"How can that be?" Neram asked.

"Why are you fighting for his life and why have the Wakers given him a suspended sentence?" Ruth asked.

"We have equipment and medications that can resuscitate someone under the right conditions.

"As for fighting for him it is because of what happened to him during that period of time. He had a vision that utterly changed him. It is like he was reborn."

"I would say that he has already served his sentence," Ruth said after thinking about it for several minutes.

"What does Brin say?" Neram asked.

"Brin was one of the first people to agree," Abe replied.

"Then I will agree. The prisoner is in your hands."

"We will take care of him," Abe said.

Grandpa came up to Abe after the councils had adjourned.

"That was an inspired defense," he said.

"Yeah. I'm not claiming credit. However, I know he has changed but I think he needs time to prove it to himself," Abe replied.

"Now what are you going to do?"

"Take him back to the LP community. That is if you meant that Jax and I are permanent leaders there."

"I did and there is no argument. We'll send you startups once you have more houses and maybe some barns built."

"I'm going to ask Jax to marry me."

"Oh?"

Abe blushed. "I've always tried to hide myself from other people but that isn't working anymore. I guess you could say I'm outgrowing it. Part of that is admitting that I've fallen in love with her and her sense of humor, abilities and sheer tenacity. Unlike Brandon, however, I'm not going to start out by adopting three kids."

"That was good for Brandon but probably not so much for you. If she says yes we'll come down for the wedding."

"I'd like that. I think she would, too. Now I just have to hope I wake up more people that know how to do things like weaving and cooking. I don't and I'm betting the Gap is going to be ticked if I keep Zane and Fred."

"That will be up to you, Zane and Fred. The Gap is still doing wakeups and has plenty of chefs, especially now that Annette has a second baby to care for."

"Oh? When did that happen?"

"About two weeks ago. It's another girl."

New Community

"I found you a weaver," Grandma said as they headed back to establish the community. "Fiona is all grown up and very adept. She's staying at Chesapeake and Joe is heading down here."

"He does leatherwork as well, right?" Abe asked.

"Yes, he does. JoAn and Scot are coming. I think mostly because the want to make sure Trevor is healing."

"They have needed skills," Abe replied.

"How are you planning to announce the new community?" Grandpa asked.

"I think we'll have a meeting with a few of our council plus Nali and his council, if he has one. If he doesn't, I'm going to suggest a couple of his members."

"Oh, which ones?" Grandma asked.

"Rani and Omri."

"I don't deserve to be on a council," Omri objected. "I am a traitor."

"That is one of the things that makes you fit to be on a council," Abe said. "Thinking that you aren't worthy is appropriate. I doubt any of us feel like we're worthy and I will tell you that this will be a lot of work. It won't be a light job for anybody and the council especially."

"Why would that make me fit?"

"The way I understand what happened," Grandpa said, "is that you wanted to be leader of all your people. You felt you were better able to do the job without knowing what the job entails. It was your ego. Now you don't have that problem. You will think about what your people need not what you want."

"That is true. I did want to be leader. I didn't do a very good job when I tried though I am glad we failed."

"That's why," Abe said.

"If Nali will have me I will serve."

The hover carts arrived just after lunch. People cheered when they saw Omri was with them. Once they landed Abe asked Trevor to help set up a meeting.

"I am glad you were able to save Omri," Nali said when they went into the house. A council chamber had already been set up. "Now what are you going to do with him?"

"With your permission he's going to be on your council," Abe said.

"That is an interesting suggestion," Nali said. "What does he think?"

"He thinks he isn't worthy."

"Then I accept your suggestion. He has the intelligence. He lacked self-discipline."

"I think he's learned that lesson. If you don't already have a council I have another person to suggest."

"You've known us only a few days, how could you know more people to suggest?"

"It's probably because I've only known you for a few days. I don't have a bias yet though I'm sure I will later. I'd suggest Rani. Not only is he a good watcher he takes the initiative to do more without being asked or told."

"When did he do that?"

"When the battle was starting. One of us would probably have suggested he take up a position between the cabins and fight but he didn't need told. He just did it."

"I would agree with your assessment of him. He would have been on any list of trusted men I made."

"You may want to add some women to your council at some point. Ours has several already."

"It is a new idea but one worth considering."

Rani was surprised to find himself at the council meeting. He frowned when he saw Omri but decided not to say anything.

Grandpa was the first to speak. "I'm not going to participate much in this discussion unless I'm needed to answer a question about Waker policies. Because it is obvious that the people that created the cryo program want a community here we would like to build one. Abe and Jax will lead it.

"However we recognize that this is in your territory. The only two questions I will ask are do you agree and will you accept them as leaders of the Waker community here?"

"We expected you to take over," Nali said. "It has rankled some."

"We don't take over unless asked. What usually happens is that we form an alliance. You would still lead your community. Jax and I would lead the Wakers and those we wake up."

"I like that idea much better," Rani said. "You are far advanced and your ways are different. We will need to have some of our familiar things; our homes and so forth even while we learn."

"That is the way it has been for all of the communities," Benton said. "As you know I came from the Caves. My family and I have chosen to become Wakers but the Caves are still their own people. They have representatives at the joint council. That is something else you may want to do, but we can discuss that later."

"I believe Abe will be a good and just leader," Omri said. "If he says Jax, the woman, is his co-leader I accept that as well."

"I agree. Yes, you may build here and we will have a joint council with you for large issues. Abe and Jax are the leaders," Nali said. "Now what do we do?"

"We need to discuss a few things," Abe said. "If you have time we can go into them now."

"We have time," Rani said.

"After seeing some of the problems faced by Chesapeake and the Gap I want to build the houses around where the animals will be kept. Pastures and corrals for practice can be outside of it but they are safer inside."

"That's an excellent idea," Amaya said. "It will also make it more protected in bad weather."

"Does everybody agree? Nathan, Johnson will it be too much trouble with wiring and plumbing?" Abe asked.

"It can be done fairly easily," Johnson said. "The outer houses may have to be tied to those closest to them so we don't have to dig so much."

"We'd have to dig anyway," Amaya said. "We have to add plumbing to the barns and coops."

"That's true. Yes, that would work," Johnson said. "Nathan?"

"Couldn't be easier. I like the idea."

"Next up is preparing for winter. Nali, we plant extensive gardens but we also hunt and forage. It might be wise to do this in teams. That way your hunters can begin to learn about some of our weapons. Your cooks may want to learn how we preserve food as well.

"Do you have access to salt?"

"There is a salt lick near us, so we do have access and use it in food preservation. I agree to the idea of teams. We can do much with our arrows but hunting larger game can be dangerous that way."

"Yes, your bows and arrows are on a level with our own. Do you have slingshots?" Abe asked.

"No, we don't. I haven't seen a weapon like that before."

"We use slingshots for small game like chickens, rabbits and squirrels. We use bows for bigger birds and sometimes deer. Our guns we use for deer and larger game. Goats can be either and sheep are usually guns."

"We have not hunted sheep or goats though the women have gathered their wool."

"They are tasty," Benton said. "As are raccoons, though we do not hunt them. They sometimes raid the crops and have to be forced to leave."

"I have had raccoon, though we don't usually hunt them. It is a specialty dish from one of the southern villages," Rani said.

Hunting, gathering and building were well underway. Abe asked Jax to go for a walk with him to check out how the new community was coming together. Once they were away from other people he began to speak.

"I know we haven't known each other very long," he began, "but I feel like I've known you forever. I've felt this way a long time but having that battle, where either one of us could have been killed, makes me less afraid to say something.

"I love you. Will you marry me?"

Jax grinned. "I figured you did and I feel the same way. My heart was in my mouth when they told me how badly you were injured. Yes, I'll marry you. When?"

"Well, as Grandma and Grandpa happen to be here, soon would be good. Joe's already set up and I think Grandpa gave him a head's up. He might have something already started for a wedding."

"How could Grandpa do that? Did he know you were going to propose?"

"Well, it is customary to ask someone. Most folks who don't have a father ask him."

"You really have done this right. Let's go tell them."

Grandma grinned when she heard the news. Of course, Grandpa had mentioned that Abe was going to ask. She led Jax off to Joe's weaving and sewing room.

"I do think it works better if there's a married couple leading a community," Grandpa observed. "You know what this is going to mean, though. Grandma is going to take charge."

"I know. I don't mind. She enjoys it and if it makes her happy it makes me happy."

"How is Jax going to feel?"

"I think she's going to enjoy it as well."

Nali was told of the upcoming wedding. He smiled. "It is good to have a wife and children. It settles a man. Treat her well."

"I'd better," Abe said. "Not only are we pretty evenly matched Grandma would have my hide."

"Your people have a great deal of respect for Grandma and Grandpa. I can see why. Is there to be a feast?"

"There is if Grandma gets her teeth into it... and she will."

"We will want to bring a contribution."

"Coordinate it with Grandma. She likes to try new things and will love it."

▢

The Wakeup

Several days after the wedding Abe announced it was time to do the first wakeups.

"I've studied the notebook and there are going to be at least two people that will pose problems. One is the lead pilot. The notebook says that he is the best pilot they have for this type of copter but that he has some issues."

"What kind of issues," Grandpa asked.

"He's arrogant and misogynistic. Neither of those is going to go over well in our society."

"Please explain mis… miss… that word?" Omri asked.

"It means that he thinks men are better than women at everything but 'women's work' and that he's the best man around," Jax said. "I'm not going to like him much."

"He will learn," Omri said quietly.

"I hope so," Amaya said. "I don't deal well with either of those attitudes."

"The other party is a doctor. He seems to have a God complex."

"What is that?" Rani asked. "Men can't be God."

"No, but some doctors, particularly surgeons and specialists, think they know better than everyone else what to do and how to do it. He's not going to like me very much," Grandma said.

"I guess I'd better have the stocks built," Abe mused. "I suspect they may be needed."

"What are stocks?" Nali asked.

"They are a wooden contraption that holds a person's head and wrists so they cannot move, lie down or even sit. They seem to be very effective," Benton said.

"It doesn't take many rounds in them for those who have minor misdemeanors to figure out how to stay out of them," Grandpa said. "Please do remember that in most cases the newly awakened should have a week before they should have adapted before stocks can be used."

"Why only in most cases?" Benton asked. "Has that rule changed?"

"Yes. Every council member believes that Connor and Frank should have had stock time long before they did. It probably wouldn't have changed the outcome but it might have," Grandma said.

"When are we going to start waking them up?" Jax asked.

"The Gap says the weather is going to be clear for the next two or three days. We'll do them in batches of ten until we get to the families and we'll start tomorrow morning. The pilot will be in the first round of wakeups."

"Might as well get that out of the way," Cindy said. "The doctor will be second?"

"He'll be on another day. One personality at a time," Abe said.

After waking the first ten up Jax interviewed each one to find out more about them. The problem became immediate when she got to Samuel Tenenbaum.

"I want to speak to your leader," he told her.

"You're speaking to one of them," Jax replied. "My husband and I are co-leaders here."

"Women can't lead effectively."

"Yes, your profile did mention you held that attitude. You need to be careful with it. We have laws against discrimination and bullying."

"All right. I would like to speak to your husband."

"When he's not busy doing something else. From what I read you are the senior pilot in this group?"

"I'm the best pilot on the planet."

"Really. Remind me to show you my flight records some time. In the meantime, you need to decide if you'd like to stay in one of the houses or in the bunker."

"This program was designed so we'd sleep in the bunker."

"Your program may short circuit, depending on what it's based on. The world has changed greatly since you were put into cryo sleep."

"It can't short circuit. My orders come from the top."

"Your orders won't work that way here. Former President Merkin, the two remaining supreme court justices and the one remaining member of the joint chiefs of staff would agree with that."

"Congress won't."

"Congress doesn't exist at all. They didn't go cryo and developed a culture of their own."

"I don't believe you."

"That would be your problem, not mine. Trevor, please show this man to the bunker. He's single so the dorm is the best place for him to go."

"I don't want to stay in the dorm. I want a room."

"Even if you stayed in one of the houses you would most likely be sharing a room with other men."

"I can't wait to talk to a man about all of this."

"That will be an interesting conversation."

While Trevor went to show the pilot where he'd be staying Jax went to find Abe. He was with Grandpa.

"The notebook was correct," she told the two men. "He's both misogynistic and arrogant. He wants to talk to a man, he wants a room to himself and he says he's the best pilot in the world. He didn't like it much when I offered to show him my flight records."

"I didn't know you could fly," Abe said.

"I can fly both small planes and copters like those. As we didn't have any access to planes or copters I didn't mention it."

"How are you planning to deal with him?" Grandpa asked.

"What would you suggest?" Abe answered.

"No, for the moment I'm going to watch the situation. As the man seems to be off to find a bed in the bunker dorm, I think Jax has done a good job. Next up is your turn."

"I'd better see him now so he can have a one-two punch, then. I think I'll show him the stocks. That seemed to help Brandon and Dr. Duff."

Abe found Samuel sitting on one of the bunks glaring around him.

"I understand you wished to speak with me?" Abe said.

"Yes. I'm here to relieve you of your duties. I'm supposed to lead this group."

"That's not going to happen. Even if you were eligible to lead the hundred people in the cryo cases around you it would not make you leader here. Jax and I were appointed by the joint councils and we have their backing."

"What joint councils? I was appointed by the president and congress. I was approved by the joint chiefs."

"I'm sure Jax told you that these offices no longer exist."

"She did. So what? She's a woman. She doesn't know anything."

"Come with me."

"Where? Do I get a room now?"

"No, you'll be sharing space with other single men. There are too many people for you to have an entire room to yourself."

"There's only ninety-nine other people."

"You obviously didn't pay attention to your surroundings. Between the village and the people that have come to help set up this community there are another three hundred people with more on the way. Once your group is awake we'll be doing wakeups in the surrounding area. No room."

"Then where are we going?"

"We have laws and you are already breaking them. The things you say can get you into as much trouble as the things you do or don't do."

"There's no law like that. Plus I have freedom of speech."

"Your speech is free. The consequences are what you need to worry about. There is to be no bullying of anyone on any topic. There is to be no discrimination of anyone on any topic. Violation of those laws gets you time in the stocks. That allows you time to reflect on your attitude."

"Stocks?"

"Yes. Stocks. There they are. Jax and I are co-leaders here. We were co-leaders before we got married and are co-leaders now. Grandma and Grandpa are senior leaders of the Wakers. You might get to meet them and I recommend being very polite to them. Nali is leader of the village on the other side of the bunker.

"I understand you are a pilot and that among those who are asleep and/or are being awakened right now you're the best. That does not make you the best at everything. It certainly does not give you leadership abilities. Leaders have to communicate well, be diplomatic and negotiate agreements and disagreements among other things. You have a good deal to learn in all three areas before you're ready for even a position on my council. Have I made myself clear?"

"You've made yourself clear but I don't believe you."

"Shall I call General Mays?"

"She's the only survivor?"

"That is correct."

"She voted against me."

"I doubt Merkin wants to talk to you but I could try."

"Why would you doubt the president wanting to talk to me?"

"As he's a civilian now and happy to be one he doesn't have to talk to you. Neither do the two justices, who are civilians now… and one of them is a woman, by the way."

"What about this joint council?"

"If you want to go before them be my guest but you'll have to make your own travel arrangements which will mean my council will have to approve of you using any community resources to do so."

"Isn't there anybody left?"

"Grandma and Grandpa happen to be here at the moment but that doesn't mean they'll want to hear you."

"If I'm not going to be the leader what am I going to do?"

"That would depend on your skills and I'm not talking about flying."

"I spent so much time getting into this program I don't really have any other skills."

"Then you will be learning them. All Wakers must be weapons proficient with at least one of our weapons. You will need to learn survival skills. Until you are proficient in an area such as hunting you'll probably be washing dishes and working with the animals."

"Washing dishes is a woman's job."

"Not here. We all take turns. We take turns doing all of the 'dirty work,' including cleaning animals, working hides and so forth."

"We've gone back to hunting and gathering?"

"Not totally but it is an important part of our ability to thrive. We also barter for things we want. Those who don't have a skill usually barter time."

"How am I going to have time if I have to do all that work?"

"Unless you're on a hunting mission or it's harvest time most jobs last no more than six hours. Some jobs are all day. The chefs are all day, as are hunters and child care workers."

"You have chefs?"

"We have chefs. We eat well even if it's not often the sort of things we had before going cryo."

"What am I supposed to do now? I mean as in next."

"Your first twenty-four hours awake are a time for you to orient yourself to the changes that happened while you were sleeping. If you have trouble doing that, either because of loved ones you lost during the plague or because the adjustment is too hard we have people to help counsel you. It's best to ask though many of us who've been awake a number of years can see the signs."

"I think I'll adjust. I'm not sure I'll adjust to your rules very well."

"I imagine you will. Our women don't take anything from anybody and most of them have skills you don't have yet. Some will even be teaching you."

"Great. Feminists."

"No, people. Forget gender unless and until you fall in love."

"Are there many people like me?"

"There are but most learned not to be. Some didn't and carried things way too far. They're either dead or in jail... which we have. We also have a court system."

"So it's not all unlike what we had before."

"No, we mostly follow the Constitution and the Bill of Rights. We don't have a president but we have councils. Each community has a council and the joint council sits at Home Base, the first community we Wakers built."

"Why are you called Wakers again?"

"Because we wake people up from cryo sleep. Two other tribes gave us that name. The villages call us the Later People but that's not likely to stick."

"We've got tribes?"

"We've got six societies all allied. The LP, which is what we're calling these folks, will soon have a seat on the council."

"What are you going to do now?"

"I'm going to get ready for the other person who is going to have problems with the new way of doing things."

"I'm guessing that will be Dr. Williams. I call him Vic because it annoys him."

"Yeah, that would be him."

"He's going to want to take over the medical aspect of things."

"That won't happen. It won't happen here and it won't happen amongst the allies. I seriously doubt he has the right skillset."

"Do you have drugs?"

"Not many of the kind he'd want."

"You're right but he won't see it that way."

"He would not be the first doctor we've awakened with this problem. He may be the first to wind up in the stocks if he insults Grandma."

"Good luck."

Abe reported the conversation at the council meeting that evening.

"You're right, we won't take that kind of treatment," Cindy said. "I bet he'll end up in the stocks a time or two until he gets that into his head."

"It's possible. I showed them to him," Abe said. "Any reports on other skills?"

"Three other pilots, a chef, two nurses, two electricians and a hunter," Jax said.

"There were still people that made a living by hunting?" Nelson asked.

"Yes, though he was a high end game guide on a ranch. He thinks this will be more of a challenge and a lot kinder to wildlife."

"How kinder?"

"In some areas there are too many of some animals, particularly deer and bison. Thinning them out a little will make things easier and improve the ecosystem."

"That's true. There was a problem with deer before we went cryo," Abe said. "Is it working out better doing the wakeups ten per day?"

"Yes," Nelson said. "It gives us more time to get detailed information about their skills plus it gives them more time to get acclimated."

"Yes, the pilot I talked to took a lot of time both for me and Jax," Abe replied. "Dr. Duff, you and I will handle our doctor tomorrow. For one thing he may know of you."

"Why do you think that?"

"Because your notebook said that you were a prominent person in your field."

"My field was research mostly though I did work with the interns and residents at the hospital."

"Well keep in mind that you are the head of this community's medical department when we talk to him. Also we need to keep in mind that he's unlikely to readily appreciate Grandma."

"I didn't at first but I do now. Without her efforts a lot of people would be dead and many more suffering from lack of simple medications."

The next morning ten more people were awakened. As prearranged Dr. Victor Williams was brought to Abe and Dr. Duff.

"Dr. Duff? I read a lot of your publications," the man said. "It's a pleasure to meet you."

"Yes, though much has changed since we went cryo. Abe is our leader," Dr. Duff turned to Abe.

"What? No, that's not how it's supposed to work. If that pilot couldn't lead then it was to be my job."

"That's not how it works now," Abe said. "Also, Dr. Duff is our community's head doctor."

"Why aren't you in charge of the entire country's medical system?"

"For several reasons, including the country you went to sleep in no longer exists, nor can it. Also, Grandma is our head doctor for all of the Waker, Cave and Camp communities."

"Grandma? As in somebody's grandmother? What can she know that you and I don't?"

"Grandma is what she was called long before I was awakened from cryo sleep. While she is a grandmother she is also the person who single-handedly restarted our pharmaceutical industry due to her knowledge of plant based medicine."

"That's a bunch of hogwash."

"That's what I thought as well. I know better now. You will learn."

"I need to speak to the people that appointed us to be here and run this place."

"We ran into that question yesterday. We have the former president, one joint chief and two Supreme Court justices. According to documents found with them all are retired. The highest authority you can appeal to is the joint council. They appointed my wife and me as leaders here."

"I don't believe you."

"Let's take a walk around so you can see how things have changed," Dr. Duff said.

"Why are there so many fresh graves?" Dr. Williams asked as they got close to the village.

"Because this was the scene of a battle about two weeks ago," Abe replied.

"You haven't changed. Always resorting to violence. I must insist that I become leader."

"For your information young man the Wakers did not injure or kill anyone in the battle. They used tranquilizer guns. One of them was killed and five were wounded. Abe was on the front line and took an arrow that nearly killed him."

"Then how did so many others die?"

"Because the LP have not yet learned that violence is not the answer. They are learning that now. It will take time," Abe said. "We just met them."

"There is something else this doctor needs to see," Dr. Duff said in a quiet voice. "We have rules, courts and various means of helping people rethink bad choices in attitudes, actions and words. You see those?"

"Stocks? Why do you have stocks?"

"Because people who challenge a leader's authority without due cause wind up in them. I almost wound up in them because I didn't approve of Grandma. Then I was shown how her methods work. I also didn't approve of the leader at the Gap community. I do now. It isn't because of the stocks. I was never in them. It's because the councils know what they are doing when they appoint leaders.

"If you ever hope to lead anything you will have to learn the ways of the people that are awake now. Otherwise you won't be able to lead your way out of a produce basket," Dr. Duff said.

"We'll see. I notice you've built houses. Are those barns? What's in them?"

"Fairly soon there will be cows, sheep, goats, horses, chickens, turkeys and rabbits," Abe said.

"You're farming?"

"There are no grocery stores and no restaurants. We hunt, forage and farm for survival. There's no pre-made clothing. The sheep are a vital part of our textile industry."

"What do you eat?"

"Whatever our chefs make usually. We've got some pretty good ones."

"This is going to take getting used to."

"Yes, it's that way for everyone when they first wake up. After the rest of your group is awake we'll have a general meeting and go over the things you need to know about what's happened and going to happen."

"They aren't all awake yet?"

"No, unless it's a smaller group we find it best to only process ten people a day. Your group has at least a hundred."

"One hundred twelve with eighteen kids."

"Yes, and the kids will be the last ones we wake up. It's far better for children if their parents are awake before they are."

"We didn't think of that when we were developing the program but I can see the point."

"Now for your next question. Do you want to stay in one of the houses or in the bunker?"

"I was supposed to stay in the bunker but I can't say I like being underground that much."

"Then we'll show you the single male doctor's room in the hospital section of the houses."

"You have another hospital? What do you have to work with in it?"

"You'd be surprised. We're not as primitive as you think. Dr. Duff, will you show him?"

"Why? What are you going to do?"

"As leader here I have a lot of jobs. Right now I'm due for a shift as dishwasher."

"You wash dishes? Leaders don't do mundane things like that."

"Here everyone takes a turn at the dirty work," Dr. Duff said. "I washed them yesterday."

⁂

General Meeting

"We're going to discuss the running of our community both for Nali's village and the Waker community," Abe told the gathered people. "Between the two groups there are over six hundred people. At this point the village accounts for more people but that will change over the course of the summer. More people want to move here and we will be waking people on a regular basis.

"I have been appointed leader of the Waker community with Jax as my co-leader. I have a council set up and will be adding a few positions as I get to know people better.

"Any questions so far?"

"I object," Sam Tanenbaum said. "Half of us already had a leader set up."

"I also object," Victor Williams said. "You have no idea how to use the things you have. Your medical practice is based on a charlatan and you still fight wars."

"We have objections," Abe said. "I have already told both of these men why they are not going to be the leaders here but if someone else wishes to address the issue the floor is open."

"I would not be alive if these people did not know how to use medical equipment and medications properly," Omri said. "Grandma is a legitimate doctor. I question whether you have the skills needed to take care of people in the present world.

"The Wakers did not harm anyone in the battle we fought. They were harmed by us. We are learning to be a more peaceful people because of Abe and his leadership here. I would not accept you as an ally nor as a man of medicine."

"As a senior leader of the Wakers and a representative of the joint council I can tell you that both of you are out of line," Grandpa said. "Dr. Williams comments such as yours get time in the stocks. That's something Abe and his council has to decide but you are skating on thin ice."

"I believe that answers your objections," Abe told the two men. "Now, on to the really important stuff. All of you newly awakened will have to undergo weapons and survival training if you do not already have it. You will all be assigned to a group. Where possible that will be in your area of expertise but as has been stated before we all take turns doing the dirty work.

"Any of you with hunting experience will be going out on a regular basis to procure meat for the winter. While out you will also be foraging and looking for things that the doctors and weavers might need. Keep an eye out for herds with young because we'll probably be adding them to those that will be arriving soon from other locations.

"If you don't have an area of expertise but have an interest in one of our groups you may join it and learn whatever that craft is. If you don't have an interest you will be assigned. These communities work because we do. Most tasks are in six hour shifts.

"We have a few children already and will probably be waking up more. We also have a few teachers. After harvest school will start for our children.

"Any questions?"

"Why do I have to learn to shoot a weapon?" Dr. Williams asked.

"Because if you're out in the middle of nowhere and a wild animal is coming at you having a means of self-defense is a sensible practice," Abe replied. "As you are currently in the middle of nowhere and likely to be going further out this becomes a strong probability."

"What if I don't want to do something I'm assigned?" a woman asked.

"There may be times when that happens. Discuss the reasons for not liking it with me or Jax. Some are valid. Some aren't. If you don't do your assignment or purposely mess it up there are repercussions."

"Are we going to get to fly?" Samuel asked.

"Yes, eventually. Not right now. It may be a week before we're ready for that. The mechanics are going over the manuals for the copters as are Jax and I. After they give them a thorough checkup we'll schedule a flight.

"We'll also have to make sure any of the Caves or Camps that might see us are aware that it is us. Even with a force field an arrow coming at you is distracting."

"How are you going to do that?"

"Radio communications are already setup. A runner will be sent to the Caves, villages and Camps that don't have a radio."

"I guess you do know how to use what you have," Samuel turned and grinned at Dr. Williams.

After the general meeting Abe requested a meeting with Jax, Dr. Duff, Grandma and Grandpa.

"This Dr. Williams seems to have a problem in all areas of life, not medicine," Abe said. "I thought that particular complex only affected areas of medicine."

"It can manifest outside of that field," Dr. Duff said. "I think it may go back to your theory of some people waking up on the wrong side of the… er… case."

"That makes sense," Grandma said. "Do remember that I have been called worse than a charlatan. As with Dr. Cora and from what I hear you he will have to get over that because orthodox medicines will run out."

"I'm not sure time in the stocks would work with him," Abe said. "It will only re-enforce his notion that we are backwards people and increase his superiority complex."

"What do you think would change him?" Grandpa asked.

"I hate to say it but seeing how life really is, how dangerous it can be and how he has to be a team player and not the pitcher."

"Send him as medic on a hunting mission," Grandma suggested. "Something other than rabbits, squirrels and deer."

"I have a scout report of cattle," Abe said. "It's a mixed herd with young. They've been hunted before and the bulls made the scout know he wasn't welcome."

"Perfect. Who will you send?"

"If I wasn't needed here I'd go. Trevor's not off the sick-list yet. Thi is. I'll send Nelson, Reilly, Joe and Amaya. That way she can handle any calves and he can look for stuff to weave."

"I think you're going to need more than that," Grandpa said. "Send Sarge and Jax."

"You guys do know that someone is likely to come back injured," Abe said.

"Yes, that's always possible on any hunting trip," Jax said. "I can handle it."

"Yeah but can I?"

"You'll get used to it," Grandma said.

The hunting trip was set up for the next day. Nelson was hunt leader and met with the team before they left.

"Dr. Williams do you have a first aid kit?" he asked.

"Yes, plus a few more things we might need."

"You filled half a cart with things. Please remove them. Experience has shown us that we can get an injured party back with the items in the kits. You aren't in an ambulance because we don't have any."

The doctor muttered as he put away the defibrillator, large drug box and various other items.

"I thought I needed to know how to defend myself before I went out on a mission," he said when he got back.

"You're going to have to depend on us for that right now. Your skills are needed and hunting can be dangerous. Most of us know first aid but having a medic along is a wise precaution particularly in an area we aren't familiar with."

"Great."

After forty-five minutes the team found the herd.

"Good, we're downwind," Nelson said. "For the moment everyone please stay in the carts. When we're in position I will turn the force field off so we can fire. Amaya, you and Thi tranq four calves. The rest of you pick an animal."

"Ready," Amaya said.

"As am I," Jax said.

"Fire!"

Four bulls were down as well as the calves. The lead bull did not like this turn of events and charged. Reilly didn't have time to get his cart's force field back up and was knocked from the vehicle.

"Don't move," Nelson said. "I don't want to shoot him, he's too old to taste good. If we all keep still we might be able to outwait him."

After staring at the man on the ground and the strange carts the bull led the rest of his herd away.

"All right, Dr. Williams, you attend to Reilly while we get to work."

The somewhat shaken doctor got out of the cart and went to where Reilly had landed.

"Are you awake?" he asked.

"Yeah but I'm kind of wishing I wasn't," Reilly replied.

"What hurts?"

"It's more like what doesn't hurt. I don't think anything's broken but it knocked the wind out of me real good and there might be some whiplash."

After checking to make sure nothing was obviously broken he rolled the man over and helped him sit up.

"Are you dizzy? Any trouble breathing?"

"No, though I am shaky. I'm also real glad I was still in a cart."

"Now what are they going to do?"

"We're going to skin and clean the cattle while Amaya and Thi hogtie and load the calves."

"You've just had an accident and you're going to work? I'm not sure that's a good idea."

"Doctor, unless there's something wrong with me I came here to do a job. You need to learn how to do this job so we are going to help. You can keep an eye on me. If it looks like I'm in trouble you can call a halt."

The two men got busy with Reilly showing the doctor what to do.

"It does help that you've done surgery," Reilly said when they were done. "A lot of people are grossed out when they first start learning to clean an animal."

"It was pretty disgusting. What surprises me is that you were able to just get up and get back into the swing of things."

"We have to, doctor. A lot of people are depending on us succeeding. It's the same with any job. We have to be a team and we have to forget petty problems and look at the big picture."

"What is the big picture?"

"Feeding seven or eight hundred people all winter. Making sure they have clothes. Making sure that when the orthodox medicines run out we have backups. Keeping them warm, dry and healthy."

"That is a big responsibility."

"It's one we all share. Sharing the load makes it easier. Let's help Joe get some of those cattails. The chefs will be happy as well, the pollen cones are good eating as are the roots."

"You eat cattails?"

"We eat a lot of things. Food isn't wasted nor any other usable part of either a plant or an animal."

"I can see why I'm not the leader," Dr. Williams said in a quiet voice. "I have no idea how to do all of those things. It also hadn't occurred to me that we might run out of the medicines I know how to use. What do you use then?"

"Grandma and her team make a lot of it though each team lead knows how to make most things. She and the Gap are the only two communities with a still for making some drugs."

"I didn't know stills made drugs."

"They do. They also make essential oils that have come in really handy when there's a hard wakeup or a person with breathing problems. I know there are others but I've only used that set."

"What is a hard wakeup?"

"Some people have trouble with the cryo gas. Some sort of bad reaction. Until Alderson and Grandma came up with the kit we'd lose a lot of them. Now we get about a ninety percent survival rate."

"We never planned for people having a bad reaction to the gas. It's amazing what's been accomplished. We left everything we could but we knew it was still going to be rough restarting. I didn't realize how rough."

"What was left has helped tremendously but I can tell you we might not have made it if it wasn't for Grandma, Grandpa and her family. They carried most of us through our first winter."

"Is that why they're so respected that you can be put in the stocks for disparaging them?"

"Yes, in part. The other part is we really don't allow bullying of any sort. Freedom of speech doesn't mean freedom from the consequences of your speech."

"I guess it never did though sometimes the consequences were on the people spoken to."

"That's why we have that law."

Neram's Request

"Samuel I've made arrangements for a test flight this morning," Abe told the pilot. "I'm going to be your passenger."

"Do you get airsick?"

"Nope and I won't this trip."

Samuel took the copter up and began doing a series of moves, ostensibly testing it. Abe sat there and smiled.

"Ok, why don't you get airsick?" Samuel asked.

"Because I knew you'd test both the copter and me. Grandma gave me something to prevent it before I got aboard."

"Smart. All right, this bird is good to go."

"Has Jax ever shown you her flight records?"

"Yes, she did. I annoyed her yesterday. She's good. In some ways she's even better than I am and you don't know how it hurts to say that."

"Oh, I've had to eat my share of crow when I first heard of women teaching survival courses. I knew they could do the class; I've taught quite a few. I just didn't think they'd be good enough to teach."

"Is she better at it than you?"

"I'd say we're very evenly matched. Some things she can do better and others I can do better."

The radio on the copter bleeped.

"Copter One, go ahead," Abe said.

"You guys need to get down here. Neram's gotten a lot worse. We need to fly Dr. Williams, Brin, the council members that are here and some requested medications up to Home Base. We've also been asked to send out additional copters to pick up the leaders of all of the Camps," Jax said.

"Ten-four. Do they need either of us?"

"I'll be flying one of the copters and yes, they want you. Apparently Neram has a final request."

"Ok, touching down now, over and out."

A tense half hour later the copters began landing near Home Base. Most of the Camp leaders were a little pale and not just because of the gravity of the situation.

"Where is Neram?" Abe asked.

"He's in the emergency section of the hospital," Judge Benjamin said. "Dr. Hadon, Dr. Duff, Dr. Williams, Grandma, Dr. Walters wants you to bring the equipment and medications on the double. Brin, you and Abe lead them there."

When they arrived the three additional doctors assessed the patient.

"What have you already given him?" Dr. Williams asked.

"Foxglove extract, willow bark and garlic. Foxglove is what digitalis was made from, willow is aspirin and garlic can help lower blood pressure. I don't think he's strong enough for mistletoe. That's why I asked you to bring blood pressure medications, nitroglycerin tablets and clot busters."

"You believe he's had a heart attack?"

"I'm positive he's had a heart attack. We finally have an EKG and he has the markers. Blood tests also show markers."

"Do you want me to administer them or do you want to?"

"I'd prefer it if you did. Orthodox medications of that sort are not my area of expertise."

After receiving the medications Neram was able to rouse himself enough to speak.

"Have you brought my grandson and the leaders?" he whispered.

"Yes, we have. You need to rest now."

"There is no time. Even if this magic medicine pulls me through I am no longer able to lead. It is time for my grandson to take over. I have one final request to make of the leaders."

"What is it?" Grandma asked.

"I want each Camp to start becoming more like you Wakers. I would like all of the Camps to become Wakers."

"I will tell them what you want and allow them to come in and hear it from you. I will not allow any arguing. If they want to argue they can do it in another room."

"Agreed. I do not have the strength to argue. I also don't think they will argue overmuch."

Grandma went out to where the people were gathered. After explaining Neram's wish she told them that if they wanted to argue about it they were not to do so in his room. "He's gravely ill."

Brin and the Camp leaders heard this request from Neram's lips and then came out.

"I see nothing wrong with his request," Palos said. "We have been using several of the Wakers' innovations for two years."

"I don't like the idea of losing our own way of life," Helton said. "On the other hand without them we wouldn't be able to survive."

"What does Brin have to say?" Liam asked.

"If I am to be the leader of us all I agree with my grandfather's request. We do not have to lose anything. We can still tell the stories of our people. We will learn more about our religion from them. We will gain much."

"Then we shall do it," Helton said.

"I think you made a wise decision," Abe said. "Though I do hope Neram pulls through."

Grandma came back into the room then.

"I'm sorry. That's one wish that will not happen. Soon after you left he took a deep breath and then stopped breathing altogether. Dr. Williams tried to resuscitate him and wasn't successful."

"How do Wakers have a funeral?" Helton asked.

"It will be a very formal affair. People will talk about Neram, we will say the burial words and then a song will be played," Brin replied.

"It isn't that far from our own practices," Liam said.

"No, it is one reason we need to become Wakers. We really are one people."

Neram's Funeral

"Today we gather to bury a remarkable man," Grandpa said. "He has led his people faithfully through meeting those who the cryo team set to wake up the sleepers. He has been fair in his judgements and often gave wise counsel.

"Over the last few years he also became a friend. We shared stories of our families and our past. We made plans for the future. He will be greatly missed, not just by his own people but by the Waker communities.

"Rest in peace, Neram. You ran the course and stayed true."

Ruth was the next speaker.

"I was skeptical about whether or not the Caves and Camps could ever achieve true peace. Our ways, I thought, were vastly different.

"In one sense that was true. But in the sense that is most important it is not. We all want what is best for our people and now we all have valid concerns about those around us who remain asleep. Neram taught me that and I am grateful.

"As Grandpa mentioned Neram also became a friend. I never thought I would say that of anyone from the Camps but I have several friends from their culture and I value each one. They taught me a great deal about dignity and about myself. I didn't like all I learned about myself. I hope I am more open-minded now when it comes to others who are not like us.

"Neram, may He take you in His arms and carry you to paradise."

The last speaker was Brin.

"There was a time when I did not respect my grandfather. My thoughts were centered on glory and how to achieve it. His were not and I didn't understand.

"Through my own childish actions I came to spend time learning the value of all people. It caused me to see things differently. Life did not center around me and glory was never a positive goal. I am glad he made sure I learned that.

"I have spent many years living with the Wakers and have even become one. I see the value of how they live, not just for the material benefits but for the benefit of everyone and everything around them. I have seen that their women are equal to their men and that this is a good thing.

"I have learned to read the tiny marks and I have read the Sacred Book. Their teachings about loving even their enemies and doing good to those who cause them harm are teachings from that book.

"I have married a Waker. She is expecting our first child. When our child is born we will teach about all of these things. The child will be valued as a child not by whether it is a boy or a girl.

"I have thought about this a great deal. I have a plan that I will be putting before the councils and the leaders of the Camps that will help us adapt to the ways of the Wakers. It is what my grandfather dearly wanted and I will honor his request. It will be his legacy."

After the burial words had been spoken the flag on Neram's coffin was removed and folded. Brin accepted it with dignity, tears running down his cheeks. Each person put a symbolic shovel of dirt on the grave.

Suddenly the air was rent with the sound of a lone bugle. It played the song so often played at the end of a funeral. The simple, haunting notes filled the air just as the last of the dirt was placed over Neram's grave.

Abe sat down with Nelson, Sarge, JoAn and Scot.

"This conversation is off the record," he told them. "If one of you objects then it is off the table.

"I want Trevor to be the teacher for outdoor skills, animal care and when they're ready weapons and hover craft."

"Is he well enough? He won't show me the scars or anything," JoAn asked.

"That is pure Trevor. He's out hunting right now and he brings home kills. Not just birds, squirrels and rabbits either," Nelson said. "I think he's well enough."

"I wonder about his age," Dr. Williams said. "I don't know him well and I'm not sure I believe half the stories I've heard about what he's done."

"Oh, you can believe them," Sarge replied. "There are probably many more you haven't heard. He was one of the first to wake up. He helped wake me and my men up which included ten miles of running and five helping carry heavy crates. That was when he was eleven."

"My question is probably more to the point," Scot said. "He's a newlywed. Do you think he's going to be interested? I wouldn't have been."

"It involves things he likes to do," Abe said. "Amaya may be a big help there. I expect them to choose their best young warriors which probably means they are married and high status. We will have to make sure it's known that both of them are high status."

"How are we going to do that?" JoAn asked.

"We can start at the introduction feast. They will sit to our right at the head table. Most cultures recognize those as seats of honor."

"You might want to think of asking Joe to make them some clothing that is a little more decorated than what they usually wear. He may not wear it to hunt but when relaxing in the evening it wouldn't hurt. Also the fact that they are both on our council will help," Nelson said.

"So there are no objections?" Abe asked.

"I don't have any," Scot said. Everyone else agreed.

"We'll bring it up in council tonight then. I'm going to have Nali and his council join us."

"What if they object?" JoAn asked.

"I suspect they will," Abe replied. "Mostly because of his age. Knowing Trevor that's going to irritate him. Once they're convinced he's old enough he'll be ticked enough to say yes."

"That's a little underhanded," JoAn said.

"Not when he's the best man for the job. He would eventually say yes anyway."

"What do you want to bet he sets up his own mini council for problems in the job?" Sarge asked.

"That's fine. In fact it's probably wise. We can all probably guess who would be on it."
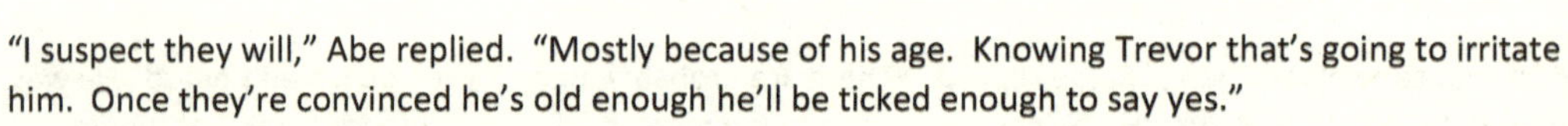

Trevor's Ordinary World

"How many do we have?" Trevor asked Amaya as he began to clean the deer he'd just shot.

"Four, each of us got one," she said while doing the same. "We also have eight rabbits."

"I guess that's good enough for one day," he said. "How's your leg, Thi?"

"It's fine. I'm more worried about your injuries. Yours were a lot more serious."

"I know. I get reminded that on a daily, if not hourly basis when we're at the community. It's why I prefer to be out here. I'm hoping that them seeing me bring in meat will eventually stop the moaning and groaning."

"I actually understand how they feel," Amaya said. "I just know better than to pester you about my worries."

"You have been an angel, my love. Marrying you is the best thing that's happened in my life."

Amaya blushed. Thi cleared his throat.

"If we're done here it's almost dinner time. Let's drop this off and get something to eat," he said.

"Now that sounds like a plan," Trevor agreed.

Once they'd dropped off their efforts of the day and cleaned up they went into the dining hall. The line wasn't that long yet so they quickly loaded their plates and found a table.

"Who do you think they're going to tag to teach the students from the Camps and the LP?" Amaya asked.

"I don't know but I don't envy them the task. I'm betting we don't know them and they don't know a lot about us. Plus the two groups hate each other," Trevor said.

"It will be a difficult job," Thi agreed. "It would be an honorable job."

"Do you want to take it on?" Trevor asked.

"No, I'm not skilled enough for one thing. I'm also of the Camps even if I am a Waker now. That would create an impossible situation."

"I'm guessing someone seasoned like Nelson, Reilly or Sarge. Nobody argues with them, they can be very frightening when they want to be," Ally said.

"I don't know," Amaya replied. "They may want someone younger and more relatable."

"Why?"

"It's hard to learn something from someone who scares you. It's not so hard when it's someone closer to your own age."

"Well that leaves me out," Trevor said. "Their warriors will be in their twenties."

"Don't be so sure. Some of ours become warriors closer to the age you were," Thi said.

Trevor's Promotion

At the council meeting that evening the subject was brought up. Nali, Rani and Omri were there to help make the decision.

"At an informal discussion earlier today we have come up with our recommendation of a teacher for the LP and Camp warriors that will soon be arriving," Abe told the council. "Our recommendation is Trevor."

"Wait, what?" Trevor said.

"You're easily our best hunter, you can control yourself in difficult situations, you know foraging, gardening and animal care frontwards and backwards. You're the logical choice."

"He is so young," Nali objected. "How can a seasoned warrior accept such a young man as his teacher?"

"He became a warrior a long time ago," Sarge said. "In fact he's due a promotion. Consider yourself a major now, Trevor."

"I appreciate the promotion…"

"What of his injuries?" Rani asked. "I know he's a warrior. He helped defend us and was seriously wounded."

"He's out hunting every day," Nelson said. "He comes back with a full game bag and usually one of the animals is large. It was deer today, right Trevor?"

"Yes, we each got one so we brought in four plus eight rabbits."

"Yesterday it was sheep?"

"Yes though we didn't skin it because Joe wanted to do it."

"If he can hunt he can teach," Rani said.

"Excuse me," Trevor said in a bland voice. "I'm sitting right here. If you wish to discuss my age, my credentials or my recent injuries shouldn't the questions be aimed at me?"

Sarge laughed, Nelson grinned and JoAn looked appalled.

"I have a few questions of my own about this job. It sounds to me like there is a lot on the line. We have two groups that hate each other. I know everyone in this room is likeminded but I seriously doubt that whoever is sent will be.

"My first question would be which of you can I turn to for help when a delicate matter comes up."

"You may consult anyone that is likely to have an answer to your question," Abe said. "That would include me, Sarge, Nelson, Reilly and your dad."

"All right, that's good to know. If you don't have a solution it can go up the chain?"

"If it's needed it will."

"You know there will be disagreements between the students."

"Yes."

"Do I follow standard Waker law or do I have a free hand?"

"I would say a little of both. I'd prefer they didn't do any stock time but even that if you have to."

"Then I accept."

Consulting with Mini Council

"Ok, guys. I can't do this without the three of you. I'll need support and I'll need advice," Trevor told Amaya, Thi and Ally.

"Are you sure you want to do this?" Amaya asked. "You weren't that keen at dinner."

"It's not really a question of what I want. While I admit being discussed as if I wasn't there was a bit rankling they have valid points. I don't mean about being the best hunter, that's debatable. The rest of it makes sense."

"Hunting prowess will be a key, at least with the Camps," Thi said. "A better weapon will be key to the LP. I also heard that you got a promotion, an increase in status."

"Yeah, I did. I've gone from scout to major which is a large jump of several ranks."

"That will be important to both of them," Ally said. "Status seems key to all of the peoples that have been awake a long time."

"Now that makes sense," Trevor said. "I was never officially in the military."

"Do you think they will bring their families?" Ally asked.

"Why would you think they have families?" Trevor asked.

"They will be high status men. Of course they will have families," she replied.

"Where will they live?" Trevor demanded.

"I heard them say that there are empty cabins in the village. Their warrior will probably stay there. The Camp warrior will probably stay with us," Thi said.

"Great. No escape."

"How do you plan to teach them?" Amaya asked, changing the subject.

"I'm thinking the shooting range is out at first," Trevor said. "It would bruise their tender dignity."

Thi laughed. "Until they're ready to handle long guns I would agree. You will have to take them in the field."

"You know that means we won't get anything."

“Maybe. Maybe not. I don't think providing for winter is now on your list of priorities. There are enough of us to do that.”

“What are they likely to do to each other? Are there limits?”

“There are limits but they will assume you do not know them. You will have to decide what you accept. They are likely to try and spoil each other's aim and they will be making comments.”

“Are they allowed to strike one another?”

“No! Not in any of the cultures.”

“Last, what if they go after Amaya?”

“That is up to you, my friend. Me, I wouldn't put up with it.”

“Oh, trust me. I won't.

Introduction Feast

"You look pretty snazzy in that uniform," Amaya said. "There's more medals, gold braid and other stuff on the tunic you almost can't see the shirt."

"Yeah, they had this ready for me this morning. It is not particularly comfortable," Trevor said.

"My dress is but the jewelry is heavy. James and Jax said I need to keep it."

"For one thing it suits you. The color matches your eyes."

"Yeah, but we're also sitting at the head table and if I remember the rules of formality at these things we're sitting in a seat that shows high honor."

Jax turned to the couple. "Everything we're doing is showing that you are both very high status among us, which is true. This first impression will be needed so you can do your job."

"I guess. I never really thought about status all that much," Trevor replied. "At least not in how much I have. I can tell the Camps and the LP put a lot more emphasis on it."

"They do. I think Abe is about to introduce your students."

Abe had risen from his place at the head table. The room grew quiet so they could hear him speak.

"Tonight we are introducing two students sent to learn about our ways, our culture and our technology. Both are esteemed warriors amongst their people. Hopefully they will find a home here.

"Blake, please stand. Blake is from Lynx Camp, which is one we have not met. He mastered the Camp bow at the age of thirteen and has been a primary hunter for them for the last ten years."

"Do we get to meet our teacher tonight?" he called.

"I will introduce him. You will meet him tomorrow.

"Cali, please stand. Yes, you may sit down Blake." It was not lost on Trevor that the two men stared at one another with hatred.

"Cali is from a village south of here. His wife, Sena has accompanied him. As they have small children she chose to stay with them this evening.

"Cali mastered the LP bow at an early age as well. He has been hunting for his people for twelve years. Everyone please welcome our guests."

When the applause died down Abe turned to Trevor and motioned him to stand. "This young man was one of the first to awaken. He has been involved in many adventures over the last seven years, including helping procure the first meal they ate on the day they woke up. He was a successful hunter before he went cryo and now is adept in all four of our weapons.

"He also has a great deal of experience in other areas that you will need to learn. Having animals has greatly improved our lives and our health. He will teach you how to take care of them. He will also be teaching you how to harvest things of importance. Let's hear it for Trevor!"

"Wow, did you see that glare between the two of them?" Amaya asked with a shudder.

"I did. I could also see that Blake is the confident kind. They are a lot harder to teach."

"You'll do fine," Jax said. "Oh, good! Dessert!"

�

Age Challenge

Trevor went into the dining room to find his students. As suspected they were sitting on opposite sides of the room. Wanting some peace while he ate he left it that way. Just as he finished Abe brought them to him.

"What are you going to do today?" Abe asked Trevor.

"Take them hunting and see what they can do," Trevor replied. "Do they already have kits?"

"Yes, Reilly gave them to them last night. Are you ready?"

"I need to get my weapons. You two follow me so you don't get lost." This did not set well with either warrior.

Once in the field Cali turned to Trevor. "Boys don't teach men. You are far younger than we are. Why isn't someone more senior teaching?"

Trevor's reply was to hit three rabbits with his sling. After putting them into his game bag he looked at Cali.

"We still shoot better."

"Let's find out. Let's also find out if you're really a hunter. Talking all of the time can drive the game away."

The three walked in silence. Trevor was tracking deer but the two warriors were too busy feeling superior to notice. Suddenly he stopped. Putting a finger to his lips he pointed.

After the three had shot at the deer the count was Trevor two, Cali one and Blake zero. The heavier Camp bows were not able to hit an animal from that distance.

"Cali, you need to put this creature out of its misery," Trevor said severely. "Always aim to kill cleanly."

"We weren't close enough!" Cali exclaimed as he did as told.

"We were close enough for me to hit two of them," Trevor said. "Now we clean them. I might as well do the rabbits while we're at it."

"Cleaning animals is a woman's job," Blake said.

"No, cleaning animals is something everybody does but usually it falls to the hunters. Do you know how to clean one?"

"Yes, I've done it before when we were on long hunts."

"Get busy. I'm going to call for a hovercart. We're not done yet and we've already got a load."

"Are you so weak you cannot carry a deer?" Blake sneered.

"No, I'm sensible enough to know that the next thing we're going for outweighs us, the three deer and the rabbits combined."

"We can't kill something bigger than a deer!" Cali said.

"Watch me."

Once they had the hovercart Trevor headed to a place that had a herd of cattle.

"If you kill one of those," Blake said, "we'll clean it. I'm that confident you can't."

After the young bull was down Trevor waved them over to clean it. The others, knowing what gunfire meant, had left.

"Is this why you are our teacher?" Blake asked with a little more respect. "They say you have a fourth weapon you can use."

"Yes, it's why. The fourth is on my belt. We don't like to kill if we don't have to. Sometimes other predators think they should get our prey. We put them to sleep for a few hours so we can finish and leave."

"How did you get so good?" Cali asked. "My bow and arrows are similar to yours yet you were able to make two kills. It is sloppy not to kill on the first shot."

"I practiced. All skills take practice. Tomorrow we will go to the range and do so. Blake, I will begin to teach you how to use our bow. As you can see the arrows go much farther."

Women

"Cali, the target is set at about the range we were from the deer. Consider the red center to be the killing spot.

"Blake, as you can tell this bow is a lot lighter and so are the arrows."

"Yes. Until I'd seen it I would not believe this twig could kill a deer."

"That is why we went hunting yesterday. As they say, "seeing is believing." Now, you see this knot in the bow string?"

"Yes."

"Put the groove in the back of the arrow just above that knot. Good. Now, lift the bow so that the arrow is level. Pull back and let it fly."

"It hit the target!"

"It did. Yours isn't quite as far as Cali's yet. As you get better I will move it back more. Keep practicing."

About an hour into the session Amaya came up to Trevor on a board to deliver a message. An outraged Blake tried to shove her off of the board. Both students were surprised at the force field.

Trevor was angry, but he didn't let that show through. He lifted Blake up one handed by his shirt front.

"First, never try to harm another person. Second, show respect to all women. Third, keep your hands off of my wife. Understood?"

Blake gulped.

Trevor set him back on the ground. "For that assault you are on ration bars for the rest of the day. I think we have had enough practice for one day. I will show you around the animals next."

"I can understand about him trying to hurt your woman but why is she treated like an equal? All of your women act like equals," Cali asked.

"That is because they are all equals. They can do the same things we can. We can do the same things they can. Some of us are more talented in an area but it is by no means gender bound. If Blake had been a Waker he'd be going to the stocks for that."

"What are stocks?"

"Those places in the middle of our community with three holes in them. The middle one is for the head. The wrists go in the other two."

"Why is he not going into the stocks? If he touches Sena he will have problems."

"If he does that to Sena bring it to the council. That is one of our jobs. As for this incident I have been given full discretion. Neither of you know our ways yet. Ration bars taste nasty but he won't go hungry. He'll also think again before attacking a woman.

"I think you picking him up by his shirt front did that. I did not think you were that strong."

"It cost me some but it was worth it. Is your wife going to eat with us?"

"No, we will eat with those from the village."

"I would prefer it in the morning if we all ate together. We can better discuss what we will be doing."

"Will your woman be there?"

"If she's not already out working with the animals."

"All right."

When they went in to dinner Trevor motioned Blake to join them. The man was looking rather unhappily at his ration bar.

"When I had this at lunch I thought 'how bad can it be?' Now I know. Are you sure it qualifies as food?" Blake asked.

"It does and it is one of the lightest of punishments for breaking laws," Trevor told him. Trevor was slightly distracted by the amount of food on Amaya's plate. "Um, do you, perhaps, have something to tell me?"

Amaya grinned. "You could say that. I can't eat much in the mornings but Dr. Duff says that's only for the first three months."

Blake looked at the two of them in confusion.

"I'm pregnant," she told him.

"And I tried to harm you!" Blake said his face pale.

"Yeah, but the force field prevented it," Amaya said.

"In the Camps that is a serious offense!"

"It is always a serious offense," Trevor said. "Male or female, pregnant or not. Now you know."

Shoveling Poop

"Ok. One of the reasons we're so successful in having plenty of food, warm clothing and other things is because we raise and care for animals," Trevor told Blake and Cali. "They provide transportation, food, feathers and fibers for weaving.

"That means we have to take care of their needs and one of those is at least once daily removing their waste from the pastures and corrals."

"Why?" Blake asked. "It doesn't need shoveled when they're wild."

"They roam over a large area when they are wild. They also suffer from some problems caused by having too much manure around. Flies and sanitation are two important ones. Not removing it can also cause a strong smell. The good news is that it is recycled as fertilizer."

"Fertilizer?" Cali asked.

"Yes. After it is treated it's used to help the garden plants grow and thrive."

"Yuck," Blake said.

"Wait till you have kids," Cali said. "If you want to talk about smells."

"Yeah but that's why you have a wife. Warriors don't deal with that."

"A wise husband knows that there are times to help his wife."

"You do women's work?"

"You will probably do the same."

"No. My wife will be properly disciplined."

Trevor sighed as the two men kept sniping at each other verbally.

"Hey, watch it!" Blake said after he was showered with a fork full of manure.

"Oops," Cali said coolly and kept scooping.

It quickly escalated until both men had measured their length in the manure.

"All right, that's enough," Trevor said. "Come with me."

"He started it!" Blake said.

"And I'm ending it. At the moment it would be wise to be very quiet."

Trevor got the two men into the showers and called Amaya over. "Here's a message for Joe and a message for Sarge," he told her. "Once you've delivered them, wait for Joe's response. It should be clothing."

By the time the men were done in the shower Amaya was back with matching outfits for them. Sarge was also waiting with a smile only an experienced drill sergeant might express.

"We have our own clothes," Cali said.

"Put it on," Trevor said. They did.

"Now. Before Sarge here teaches you how to clean the clothes you messed up I want to show you something."

Meekly the men followed Trevor to the nursery.

"Look through the window and tell me what you see," he commanded.

"Little kids," Blake muttered.

"Are they arguing? Throwing things at each other? Calling each other names?"

"No."

"If three and four year olds can keep from doing that surely people as old as you can. Now. Go clean your clothes."

"But my wife…"

"Is not going to have to clean up that mess you made. I'll see you at dinner."

Trevor sat down and closed his eyes. It was hard to believe that these were two of the finest warriors available. Someone sat down beside him.

"I understand you've had a difficult day," Abe said.

"Our children are better behaved."

"Where are they?"

"Learning to wash their clothes with Sarge. Cali was all for having wife do it but she didn't make that stinky mess."

"What are they wearing now if they have to wash their clothes?"

"Matching outfits Amaya got from Joe. They have so much ethnic pride they can't see the bigger picture."

"This should prove interesting," Abe said with a smile. "You're doing a good job. By the way, fishing contest tomorrow. I suggest you separate the combatants."

"I'll be happy to."

�

Fishing Contest

"What is a fishing contest," Blake asked. "Is it a competition?"

"You could say that. We all catch fish. There's usually a winner for the most caught and the biggest fish. Today you'll be with Thi. After yesterday I think keeping the two of you apart for a few hours is a wise idea."

"I will like that. He is from the Camps."

"He will tell you that he is a Waker. Good luck."

Trevor turned to Cali. "Have you ever fished before?"

"No but I have had food from the water. One of the southernmost villages is on the coast of a great salty water and they bring in all kinds of food."

"So you guys go all the way down to the gulf of Mexico," Trevor mused.

"You know of the great salty water?"

"I have been swimming in that great salty water. Back to fishing. I see you already have a pole set up. As nobody has been catching them the fish are probably fairly stupid when it comes to hooks and bait. You put some bait on the hook and then drop it into the water." Trevor demonstrated and almost immediately had a bite.

"Now what do you do?"

"Now I wrestle it out of the water, take it off the hook and put it in this bucket of water and go again. While I'm doing that you try."

The two fished quietly for a while. Cali caught a few and was delighted. Trevor, as usual, was catching many.

"I have not been as far as the great salty water," Cali said. "What did you call it?"

"The Gulf of Mexico. I have been many places you haven't and had to deal with things you probably never will. That was all before cryo sleep. Now, keep in mind that fishing is a quiet sport."

Further up the small river they heard a loud splash. Trevor sighed, knowing who most likely fell in.

"At least it won't scare the ones in our area away," he muttered.

"At a guess Blake fell in. As a second guess it's because he didn't listen to Thi."

About that time the triangle was rung.

"What does that mean?"

"The fishing contest is over. Let's go see who won and why Blake had a dunking."

Blake was sitting in a patch of sunlight to let his clothing dry. "I almost caught the biggest fish," he told Trevor. "It was strong and pulled me in."

"Was Thi trying to get you to use a gaff to haul it in?"

"He had a clawed stick thing."

Thi came up at that point. "Which he would not use nor would he listen. It was a huge catfish."

Trevor shook his head. "Let's see who won."

"As usual," Abe said, "Trevor wins for most fish caught. The largest fish goes to Nelson."

Introduction to the Slingshot

"Today I'm going to introduce you to the slingshot," Trevor said. "It is probably my favorite weapon, especially for small animals. It's a simple weapon but it takes a great deal of practice to master."

"If you have a bow and a long gun why use a sling?" Cali asked.

"It's light, easy to stick into a pocket, it's renewable, the balls don't break at inopportune moments, it's silent and it's not overkill."

"Metal arrows don't break."

"Bow strings break and I've seen what happens when a metal arrow hits something harder than it is. Are you ready?"

After showing Cali how to use the sling he turned to Blake. When both men were practicing he stepped back to watch.

"Ouch, watch where you're aiming that thing!" Blake said, rubbing his shoulder.

"Oops," Cali said.

A few minutes later Blake deliberately spoiled Cali's aim.

"That's enough, children," Trevor said. "Ration bars for both of you. Let's head for the garden."

When they got to the first field both men dropped their jaws in surprise.

"This is massive," Cali said.

"This is one of several. This is what will keep us well fed through the winter and early spring. There are strict rules in the gardens. Breaking them gets you no rations and stock time. I can't change that and I wouldn't try.

"Do not waste food. Do not pick under ripe food. Do not throw it at each other. Concentrate, for once, on doing this right."

"Wasting food is not allowed," Blake said. "I pledge you that I will not."

"It takes food out of the mouths of our women and children. I, too, pledge," Cali said.

What followed was several hours of relatively peaceful work gathering tomatoes and squash. As they took the results of their labors to the kitchens to be processed, Cali said, "That is a lot of hard work."

"It is but it's worth it."

"Why do you have so much?" Blake asked.

"How many men, women and children are in your Camp?" Trevor asked.

"Four tens plus a few."

"Wakeups have been happening while I've been teaching you. There are already five hundred, fifty tens of people here and there will be more by winter."

"Are my people included in this?" Cali asked.

"Those who help get their share. Your people have been working in the gardens alongside of ours. They've been hunting with ours."

"It is good to know."

"Tomorrow I am going to introduce you to camp cooking and hovercarts. We've been asked to go along with Joe on a foraging trip the day after. He will be lead. After that we will go on our first hunt."

�

Cooking, Carts and Cotton

"Today you are going to cook your own lunch," Trevor told his two students.

"Only women cook!" Blake said.

"No, we have two men as lead chefs. I don't know about you but women are not always on an extended hunting trip. What do you eat then?"

"Dried food," Cali said.

"Yuck. I'd rather have a nice, tasty spit roasted rabbit. That is what you are going to make.

"As you can see the fire for today is already lit. The rabbits are already prepped and all you have to do is cook them. You each have a fire and if I catch you breaking fire protocol in any way…"

The two men concentrated on the job at hand and finally sat down to eat the rabbits they had cooked.

"Now this is a man's meal," Cali said.

"Oh, women like it as well," Trevor said. "It was our first meal when we got out of the cryo cases."

After they'd eaten and cleaned up their mess, another fact they didn't like, Trevor took them to the hover shed.

"This is what we're going to do. I am going to show you the basics of driving the cart and then you will each have a turn driving. It would be wise of you to listen and observe."

As Trevor half expected the two spent the instruction time bickering over the fishing contest. After making sure the force field was on he had Cali take over driving. They bounced off of a tree.

"What happened?" Cali asked, shaking his head.

"You hit a tree. The force field prevented the cart from being damaged. Your turn, Blake."

Blake smirked but soon found himself in a wild ride going up, down and in circles.

"Now," Trevor said when the cart came to a halt. "You spent the entire time I was explaining the few things you need to know arguing. When you went to drive you made every mistake in the book. Watch me. Pay attention. This is real life."

The two men watched as Trevor skillfully maneuvered the cart. When they tried again they both made a credible attempt.

The next morning they were out early. Cali yawned. "I'm only up this early if we are hunting," he said.

"I'm not lead on this," Trevor replied. "Joe is."

"Does that mean if we do something wrong he decides what happens?" Blake asked.

"The entire council decides. I would behave if I were you."

When they got to the site Joe had chosen Trevor and his students were assigned to pick cotton. Trevor pulled out gloves and offered them to his students, who refused. Shrugging he pulled his on.

"Ouch!" Blake said when he reached for a fluffy ball of cotton. "It bit me!"

"No, it didn't. You got scratched by the bole," Trevor said as he continued to pick.

"My fingers are bleeding," Cali complained.

"Would you like to put the gloves on now?" Trevor asked.

"Is that why you are wearing them?" Blake asked.

"Yep. This is not my first round of gathering cotton, or any other material for weaving. I knew about the boles."

"Our women gather this," Cali said. "They don't wear gloves and I have never heard them complain."

"I seriously doubt it's because it doesn't hurt them," Trevor said. "Something you might want to think about."

?

Camp Out Showdown

"Do you have everything?" Trevor asked Cali and Blake.

"I think so. We don't take anywhere near this much stuff with us when we go on a long hunting trip," Blake said.

"We don't have to and some of it we didn't have at first. It's just more convenient.

"Now listen to me. Hunting is serious business. You could seriously hurt someone with all of these weapons. Do not aim at each other. Do not accidentally hit each other with the slingshot. I'll be the only one with a long gun and a tranq gun."

They didn't hit each other but over the course of the day they did spoil each other's aim. Finally Cali had enough and punched Blake in the face. This started an all-out fight. Trevor got between them and physically separated them, getting punched several times himself.

When the two combatants were sitting on the ground wiping blood off their faces Trevor took his shirt off.

"I ought to send the two of you back to your communities as the lowest ranked men of all of your people. Hitting people is not acceptable in any way. What do you have to say for yourselves?"

"What happened?" Blake said, his face pale. "How did you get so severely injured?"

"There was a battle at the village. I was hit in the chest and the back."

"How did you live?" Cali asked.

"I almost didn't. None of the Wakers injured or killed anyone. We used the tranq guns to put them to sleep. One of our people was killed. Five others, including me, were injured."

"We have not treated you well."

"No, you've been too busy seeing your differences and trying to sabotage each other's efforts. That has got to stop. If I tell the council what you just did you will be sent back as I said. Do you want that?"

"No," the two men said simultaneously.

"Then you are going to prove that to me right now. You guys punched me in the injuries. They are hurting. You will set up camp, cook dinner and clean up the mess. We can discuss watches after dinner."

Trevor watched as the two men set up tents, built a fire and prepared the meal. They served him before getting their own food.

"Which is better?" he asked. "Working together or obstructing each other?"

"Working together," Blake said.

"Then let's continue to do so."

⸮

Bison Hunt

"You two have been practicing for three weeks with the long gun," Trevor told his students. "You're doing very well.

"Tomorrow there is going to be a bison hunt. The council has asked if you want to participate. If you do I will explain how it's going to happen and what you have to do. Your lives will depend on you following instructions."

"I have seen bison but we rarely hunt them," Cali said. "They can be dangerous animals."

"I have seen them but we leave them alone. Our arrows are not suitable," Blake said.

"Are you going?"

"Yes."

"All right. We are going to stand in an inverted V formation. Those who have hunted bison before will be closest to the front. In this case that includes me so you two will have to look out for each other.

"Anyone who gets into trouble for any reason needs to move into the center of the V. Going outside of that is likely to get you trampled to death. Got it?"

"Got it."

The next day there were several nervous hunters towards the back of the formation.

"Those animals are big," Blake said. "One would feed an entire Camp for a month."

"They will also provide warm clothing or bedding," Cali said. "They're starting."

Everyone got ready to aim and the bullets flew. Blake stepped slightly outside the V. Cali grabbed him back just before a bison ran over him.

"Thanks," Blake said. "You saved my life."

"It is what hunting partners do. You'll probably save mine soon."

Twelve bison were killed. Cali and Blake were pleased that they each got one.

"Let me guess," Cali said to Trevor as he came up to them. "We get to skin and clean them now?"

"Yes, and some butchering. They are too heavy otherwise."

"Butchering you will have to teach. By now we've skinned and cleaned enough large animals that we should be ok there."

"That's good to hear. This hunt means there will be no hunger during the winter. It is an important one."

"Will the village get a share?" Cali asked.

"They took out four and will keep them."

⁇

Hunting Party

"Day after tomorrow we're going on an overnight hunting trip," Trevor said. "Thi, Ally and Amaya are coming. I'd like Sena to come. Young children spend time in our care facility when the parents have to be away so the kids will be fine."

"I will ask. If there are other women she may wish to."

The six headed out early in the morning.

"We're going quite a distance today," Trevor said. "It will still be early afternoon when we get to our camping spot but we'll hunt tomorrow. Amaya wants to bring in some lambs and kids and they don't stay asleep that long."

"Why do you wish to bring home living animals?" Sena asked.

"They provide us with milk and the sheep provide wool as well. We use the milk in cooking and in making cheeses."

"I have grown fond of some cheeses," Cali said.

"We have had many interesting things to eat," Sena said. "If keeping animals helps provide them I would like to learn how to care for them."

"That is a lot of work, Sena. I've helped out. Are you sure?" Cali asked.

"Yes, I'm sure. Bearing children and raising them is also hard work. I see how the Waker children are thriving and I want that for our children and for our people."

"I'll be happy to teach you as long as I'm allowed to do it," Amaya said. "I doubt I'll be able to later on in pregnancy."

"Ally is also expecting," Thi said with a grin. "She helps with the animals though I fear it is too hard."

"Don't worry. If either of us don't stop on our own the doctors will make us stop," Amaya said. "Dr. Duff is firm on that. In the meantime the exercise will help make childbirth easier, so they say."

The next morning they tracked down the sheep first.

"There are quite a few older lambs," Amaya said. "If we're also getting goats I'll only take four."

"If we find them we are," Trevor replied. "We can get four sheep as well."

"Are we going to skin them?" Ally asked.

"No, Joe wants to do that. All we have to do is clean them."

After taking care of the necessary details they moved on. "Those kids are so cute!" Ally said.

"We'll get four of them and six adults," Trevor said.

When they returned home there were accolades both for the new livestock and the sometimes hard to get sheep and goats.

☒

More Construction

"Have you guys ever wondered how we build the houses and have all of the stuff we do inside them?" Trevor asked Cali and Blake.

"I have," Cali said.

"So have I. It seems like magic," Blake said.

"It's not magic and it is a lot of work. Abe wants to start building an outer circle of houses so we have room when we wake up more people. We only have one empty house right now. Do you want to help?"

"We do," Blake said. "Why are they being built in a circle?"

"Two reasons. It makes wiring and plumbing easier and the houses with sentries keep animals and people from trying to get our livestock."

"I have wondered where the water goes when you are finished with it," Blake said. "Does it just go into the ground?"

"No, there is a water treatment plant under the bunker. The water is cleaned and then goes out into the creek."

"I never thought you could clean that out of water," Blake replied.

"It can be done and actually has to be. The communities that don't have a bunker with treatment plant have had to build them. The Gap community is doing that this summer."

"I never thought of that. This is hard work," Cali said. "I thought building a cabin was hard. You have so many small pieces."

"Yes, we're framing the building now. As we get done with a section of framing you can see that the plumbers and electricians are beginning to do their parts."

"That is what the water and the electricity flow through?" Cali asked. "Clever to have them inside the walls."

By the end of the day three more houses were framed, wired and plumbed. "I know we didn't do much but I do feel proud of what got done," Blake said.

That evening Trevor gave his first full report to the council.

"I haven't said anything thus far because at first things did not go well," he said. "The two of them were constantly bickering and trying to make each other look bad.

"It all came to a head when they got into a fist fight. After I got them separated I threatened to send them home as the lowest ranked males of all of their people."

"How did they react to that?" Abe asked.

"They were a little distracted by my recent injuries. It was the first time they ever saw me with my shirt off. When they realized the commitment I had made to this they decided that they should probably work together like they were supposed to from the beginning."

"Are they doing it?" Jax asked.

"Yes, they are. In fact, Cali saved Blake from getting trampled on the bison hunt."

"Well done, Trevor," Scot said.

Harvest

"You like tired, Cali," Trevor said at breakfast. "Are Sena and the kids ok?"

"Yes, but I am tired. One of the cabins had sparks coming out of the chimney. These are the oldest cabins of all of our people. If a spark catches a roof on fire the whole village is in danger."

"What are they going to do about it?" Blake asked.

"The fire is out now and they are sweeping the chimney. That should stop it from sparking."

"Are you going to be able to work today? Trevor asked.

"I've been up all night before when one of the children has been ill. I'll be fine."

"Ok. Today we start the harvest. We'll be getting the root vegetables, the hard squashes, corn and clearing the gardens of the rest of the produce. Another team will be cutting grains and hay."

"Why are you closing down the gardens?" Cali asked.

"It's time. Everything is ready and at harvest everybody helps, even the older children."

"I must tell Sena. The children like your daycare and they are already learning a great deal. She will want to help."

The four joined hundreds of others harvesting crops. Those who weren't harvesting were busy preserving what was brought in. It took nearly a week to bring all of the food grown in and prepped for winter.

"That is a lot of food," Sena said. "We each received a share for our winter supplies."

"It tastes really good in the middle of winter," Trevor said. "Especially peas."

"Those are a spring vegetable!"

"Yes, but we can them so we can have them in winter."

"What are in those jars?" Blake interrupted. "It looks like a brown liquid."

"It's not quite a liquid, more like a syrup," Trevor replied. "I'm guessing we have someone who knows how to make molasses. That's what it looks like."

"What is molasses?" Sena asked.

"It is a sweet syrup that can be used as a topping, in cooking and even to make candy," Trevor replied. "Grandma makes it every year but I don't think any of the other communities do. That's going to be a good trade item."

Disaster

"LP this is the Gap," Reilly was on radio duty.

"Go ahead Gap."

"This is Jackie. Jeannie says to tell you a bad windstorm is coming. It should be dry, just high winds. She says batten down the hatches whatever that means."

"Understood, Gap. I'll tell folks to get ready. LP out."

Reilly sent a runner to Abe who came to the radio post to see if there were more details.

"It is highly unusual for a dry windstorm in this part of the continent," he told Reilly. "Something really weird must have happened to the weather for that to happen."

"After everything is brought in or tied down maybe ask Nali or Cali. They'll know if it's happened before."

"Good idea."

It didn't take long to get the animals in the barns and everything secured. When that was done Abe asked Cali about the wind.

"It is a rarity for it to be dry but it does happen. Most think it is a prediction of a harsh winter."

"Good thing we all have a lot of food," Abe said.

"Yes, it is."

It started in the night. The sentries saw the glow even before someone from the village thought to get the Later People to help. They rang the alarm, not certain what was on fire but something was.

"Come on, Blake. The village is on fire. We have to go help."

"Cali and his family are in there!"

"Yeah. Here, take this respirator. It should help us breathe."

"That wind is still howling," Blake yelled. "This is going to be bad."

"Yes, it is. Look, there's Cali carrying Sena. We should go in and get the kids."

The first two were easy to find and Trevor had Blake take them outside. He found the baby on the bed and the other little girl hiding behind a chair. He grabbed both and headed out of the cabin. He was barely clear of the smoke before he passed out from inhaling so much of it.

"They did think to wear respirators," Dr. Duff said as he worked on Trevor. "I guess they didn't know they didn't have filters in them. Should I intubate him?"

"Only if you want a fight on your hands," Scot said. "Put him on oxygen...and use a cannula. He hates masks."

Aftermath

"Why am I in the hospital and why does my throat hurt," Trevor croaked.

"Maybe because you ran into a smoke filled building that was burning down around you?" Amaya asked with a touch of sarcasm.

"I had on a respirator!"

"Which didn't have a filter. It must have had some protection. Dr. Williams said with the amount of time you spent in there it could have killed you. What were you doing?"

"I had to find Cali's other two kids. One of them was hiding. Are they ok? What else happened?"

"The entire village is a total loss. By the time you got there ten had burned down and over twenty were well engaged. Sarge tried to save the rest but in the end he had to make sure the forest didn't catch on fire as well. That they did prevent."

"Did we lose any people?"

"No, everyone got out. There are a few other cases of smoke inhalation and a couple of pretty bad burns but in that department we got off pretty light."

"I'm guessing they lost everything, clothes, blankets and all the food they'd stored. What are they going to do?"

"They've moved into the three houses just finished. We'll need to build a couple more. Abe says that with a few more good hunts, including a hog hunt, we should be fine."

"Has anybody told Grandma?"

"With her grandson both a hero and on the injured list? Of course!"

"What's she going to do."

"She didn't say but she said they'd come up with something."

Grandma to the Rescue

"LP how many aircraft do you have?" Grandma said on the radio.

"Five along with pilots," Jax answered.

"So it will take more than one trip each. When can you have them here at Home Base?"

"It's a half hour flight, when do you want us and why?"

"As soon as you're ready and you'll see."

Jax let Abe know then went to the hospital section to see how the patients were doing.

"Bored," Trevor said, his voice no longer hoarse.

"Well, I have a feeling Grandma is up to something. How about if all of you come out, enjoy the sunshine and watch to see what she's up to?"

"Sena may not want to leave the children," Cali said. "She was angry with me for saving her first."

"Josh and Jaimie aren't busy right now. They can come out and keep them entertained if that's needed. They may just want to cuddle you."

"It would not be the first time and that was a scary experience," Cali said.

Sena agreed and soon Trevor, Amaya, Blake, Cali and Sena were seated under a shade tree in full view of the bunker/hanger. They watched as the five copters took off and again when they landed two hours later.

The first trip brought mostly people and equipment. It also brought Grandma and Grandpa. Jax got out two more chairs and they sat down with the others. Then the copters took off again.

"What's going on?" Trevor asked Grandma.

"I called in the cavalry," she replied. "I'd still be up there directing it but they said the news took a lot out of me and I've been ordered to rest. I figured I'd rest better here where I can see you're still in one piece."

"Yeah, I'm in one piece. I can tell you that I have no desire to be a fireman."

"That's a good thing. It was smart of you to put on a respirator first. Why they would be minus filters is beyond me."

"Me, too. Who else did you bring down?"

"A construction team, a hunting team, Henrietta, James, Andrea and Eileen. You should have enough housing and furniture in the next couple of days. The hunters will bring in the hogs and anything else they find as a good deal of the food supply was lost in the fire."

"That will help a lot," Amaya said. "What are they going to get now?"

"Pretend it's Christmas and wait to see what comes off the copters. Brandon and a group from there are on their way. I don't know what all they're bringing other than some saltpeter, both prepared and unprepared."

"We could use that next planting season," Amaya said. "I hope he brings some pink salt."

"He might. They went and got more over the summer."

"How is Brin holding up?" Trevor asked.

"He's doing quite well. There were a few problems between the LP and the Camps but they're getting it squared away."

Both Blake and Cali squirmed a little.

"Were you two a problem?" she asked, having noticed.

"We did not get along in the beginning," Blake said. "Trevor changed that."

"That is a good thing. Brin has decreed that any Camp member in this program that is sent home before its completion will be the lowest status for the rest of his life."

Blake flushed.

"I didn't know that but I told them that's what would happen to both of them," Trevor said. "Glad to know there was backup."

"Do I want to know what happened?"

"No, it's over and done with. They have more than proved themselves as did Thi, who is sitting over there like he didn't do anything to help. I'm betting Ally gave him as much of an earful as Amaya did me."

"Yeah because he didn't even put on a respirator," Ally said with some vehemence.

"He probably didn't know where or what they were," Grandma said gently. "It was very brave of him. You, Amaya and Sena should be proud not ringing a peal over your husbands."

"Can't I be proud, mad and scared at the same time?" Amaya asked.

"Honey that's going to happen your whole married life. What you have to do is learn to let go of the mad once you see he's safe. Please remember; turnabout is fair play. If you do something dangerous, even if it's the right thing to do, he's going to feel the same way."

"I hadn't thought about that but what am I likely to do that's dangerous?"

Grandma looked at Amaya's abdomen which was already beginning to show signs of pregnancy.

"Oh."

"You do a lot of very heavy work with some very large animals," Grandma said.

"I am proud of Cali," Sena said. "But I don't understand why he took me out first."

"You don't?" Grandma asked.

"I have lived to adulthood; the children have not."

"That makes sense to you as a mother. Obviously to Cali you are the most important. I understand he was headed back in to get the kids when these two heroes came out with them."

"He was."

"Then I would try and think of it from his perspective and love him as much as he obviously loves you."

Sena looked at Cali and he nodded. She reached out with the hand not holding the baby and held his tightly.

"I think they're going to need a cradle again soon," Ally said in an undertone to Thi.

"That would be a very good thing," he replied.

At that point the copters began arriving again. Boxes, bundles and bales were being unloaded. Some Trevor could figure out but not what was in the boxes.

"Ok, it's Christmas but I can't go open the presents. What are all of those?" he asked.

"Hides, furs, clothes, cloth, yarn, thread and a lot of stuff for the weavers. There are also a lot of the things they need to turn all of that into something useful. Henrietta saw to it so I'm not sure which is what but there are five copter loads."

"Where is it coming from?" Amaya asked.

"A lot of it is donations. The Caves and the Camps take fires like this very seriously, and for good reason. Aside from the donations everyone who had planned to come and trade with you chose to donate their trade goods instead. They knew you really wouldn't have anything to spare in trade."

Tears filled Trevor's eyes. "Some of the northern communities don't have that much to spare," he said.

"They didn't before but with all the trades with us and the skills they've been learning they are thriving," his grandmother said. She was pleased at the reaction but didn't want to embarrass him.

"I'm glad they're doing so much better."

The next load looked to be toys and other bundles.

"You may or may not have the resources to make presents for the children," Grandpa said. "I arranged this part. Everyone got involved. Ruth and the Camps sent folks to help."

All of them, except Blake, had tears in their eyes. He looked at them with curiosity.

"At Christmas we have a huge party," Trevor explained. "We celebrate the birth of Jesus and we give each other presents. Community members spend a good deal of time making special things to give to the children without them knowing who it comes from."

"With all that was destroyed by the fire we might not have had enough wood or other materials to make them, though with all of these donations and the way those workers have already started hauling in wood we might," Amaya said.

"That is a significant gift," Blake said. "All of this is showing our community great honor. Why?"

"Because we're all family, really," a familiar voice behind Trevor said. The next thing he knew there was a pet carrier in his lap.

"Linda sent these for you and Amaya, knowing how much you both like cats. They are unrelated so can breed," Brandon said.

"Oh, look how gorgeous!" Amaya said. "Is that Naranja?"

"Yes but the male hasn't decided to answer to any name we've tried," Brandon said.

"Have you tried Merlin?"

"Mrrp?" the black cat said.

"No, and I think he now has a name," Brandon laughed.

While Trevor and Amaya petted the cats they watched Brandon's folks unload their carts.

"I don't think we're going to be cold or hungry this winter, no matter how bad it gets," Cali said. "It is a relief to know my wife and children will be well."

The last copter load brought several more people. Tony, Noah and Andrea were among them.

"That's my cue," Brandon said.

"Are we having a feast?" Amaya asked.

"It's my understanding you didn't get to have a harvest feast," Grandma said. "As I've been strictly ordered to stay out of the kitchen I brought re-enforcements. Also someone else wanted to come."

Brin and Cindy came up to the group and sat down.

"I wanted to come and tell you all how well you did during the fire. Even though you are Wakers, you will also always be of the Camps Thi and Ally. The three of you have gained much status.

"I am told that you are learning many things and the most important one is to get along with all people. I look forward to hearing of your learning to read and the other classes taught by the Wakers, Blake."

The three murmured their thanks.

"Ok, show's over guys," Grandpa said. "Trevor, the four of you that were in that fire should probably take a rest. If half of what your grandmother has been up to happens you'll be exhausted by the end."

"I could do that," Trevor said.

⍰

Harvest Feast and Speeches

"There is a lot of food," Sena said as she ate her second course. "When we have feasts everything is served at one time."

"Grandma likes it this way," Trevor told her. "She was like this even before cryo."

"Nali is getting ready to speak," Cali said.

"I would like to talk about something different today," Nali said when the room had quieted. "I could speak of bravery and others will. I wish to speak of humility.

"When this program of teaching both the Camps and our people at the same time I had two problems. I thought the young warrior who would be teaching was too young. I was wrong.

"I also have grown up with a dislike of the people of the Camps. I thought they were not smart enough to take part and certainly not brave enough. Again, I was wrong.

"Yesterday two warriors of the Camps and Trevor rushed in to burning cabins and saved lives. It nearly cost them their own. I have learned that we are all people. The Camps are not less than our people and we all have much to learn from the Later People, who call themselves the Wakers.

"Thank you."

"Wow," Thi said. "I knew these people didn't much like us. I didn't know the extent. I'm kind of glad he's learned that lesson. Maybe the rest of them will."

"I suspect his change of attitude is not the only one," Sena said. "Mine had already changed but the women have all talked about how brave all of you were."

"I would agree. Oh, nice. Someone made Grandma's soup," Trevor said.

"Yes, and Brin is about to speak," Blake said.

"Thank you, Nali. I have learned a great deal from you in the last few hours. It is true that our peoples have a tradition of dislike and mistrust. I have learned much from the Wakers, as did my grandfather. This program was his wish; his legacy.

"I am proud of the people of the Camps who are living here. They are helping fulfill that legacy. As for bravery I have learned that a member of your people saved Blake's life on a bison hunt. That is not a small thing though he made it out to be.

"It is good that we are learning to work together. It will make us all a stronger and better people."

"If you had asked me when I first met him if Brin would ever make a leader I would have said no," Thi commented. "He was a spoiled brat. Now I think he may become a better leader than even his grandfather."

"He has worked hard to get where he is," Grandpa said. "All of you have."

Abe rose to speak next.

"Our heroes are probably getting tired of being told how brave they are," he began. Trevor grimaced in agreement. "I'd like to talk about gratitude.

"I'm grateful everyone survived the fire. We could easily have lost entire families. Before cryo it happened a good deal. I'm grateful the fire didn't spread. With the wind blowing the way it was it could have burned down a large section of forest.

"I'm also grateful for the gifts we have been given to make sure we get through the winter. We will have enough food, clothing and other essentials to make it through the winter. Without the generosity of other communities it would have been tight.

"I am grateful that we have a new sense of community. That has taken time but it has now also been literally tested by fire. It brings joy to my heart."

"I'm grateful, too," Trevor said. "Especially when it comes to a good beef roast."

Grandma laughed and got up to speak.

"On behalf of our community and the others who have donated items, you are welcome. We know that should something bad happen elsewhere you will return the favor.

"I am proud of all of you. It takes a lot of courage and self-discipline to accept that something new is also something better. It takes work to learn new things. You have worked hard. If you keep going you will find the rewards are very sweet... almost as sweet as what Noah is about to serve for dessert."

"I don't know what this is but whatever it is I'm going to learn to make it," Sena said as she ate chocolate candy. "I am glad we have come to know you Later People."